THE
ART OF
DUMPSTER
DIVING

TURNER PUBLISHING COMPANY
Nashville, Tennessee
www.turnerpublishing.com

THE ART OF DUMPSTER DIVING
Copyright © 2019 Jennifer Anne Moses
All rights reserved

Cover design: Tree Abraham
Book design: Karen Sheets de Gracia

Library of Congress Cataloging-in-Publication Data
Names: Moses, Jennifer Anne, author.
Title: The art of dumpster diving / Jennifer Anne Moses.
Description: Nashville : Turner Publishing Company, 2020. | Summary: In Crystal Springs, Louisiana, when sixteen-year-old James finds his mother lying in her bed, dead, he tries to run the household by himself, hiding his mother's death from the authorities, caring for his little brother, and scrounging for food until things become increasingly desperate.
Identifiers: LCCN 2019025026 (print) | LCCN 2019025027 (ebook) | ISBN 9781684424627 (paperback) | ISBN 9781684424634 (hardback) | ISBN 9781684424641 (ebook)
Subjects: CYAC: Family problems—Fiction. | Friendship—Fiction. | Louisiana—Fiction.
Classification: LCC PZ7.M84734 Ar 2020 (print) | LCC PZ7.M84734 (ebook) | DDC [Fic]—dc23
LC record available at https://lccn.loc.gov/2019025026
LC ebook record available at https://lccn.loc.gov/2019025027

9781684424634 Hardcover
9781684424627 Paperback
9781684424641 eBook

PRINTED IN THE UNITED STATES OF AMERICA

19 20 21 22   10 9 8 7 6 5 4 3 2 1

THE ART OF DUMPSTER DIVING

JENNIFER ANNE MOSES

TURNER
PUBLISHING COMPANY

For Sam and Jonathan

1

WHEN WE WERE WE

It wasn't always just Danny and me. First, it was Danny and me and Mamma and Daddy and Grandma and my older sister, Lila, who was really my cousin. You could tell by looking at her that she wasn't our real sister. Danny and me were on the scrawny side, shy and quiet, with too many freckles and flat hair the color of Cheerios. Lila was a redhead, with a flaming mass of curls that she wore every which way. She had a million friends who she invited over all the time, who, along with the millions of church ladies that Grandma had over all the time, added up to a full house. We even had a pair of parakeets, Sonny and Cher. Sonny was green as a sour apple lollipop, and Cher was the deep blue of nightfall, with black specks on his head. They sang all day long and wouldn't shut up until it was night and we draped a towel over their cage. Those were some smart birds. Mainly all they said was *tweet, tweet*, but they knew some English too. You never knew when they were going to say something meaningful, like *I love you* or *Pretty bird* or *Thank you*, or when they were going to stick strictly to bird language.

Our house on the corner of Elm and Twenty-Third Street in Crystal Springs wasn't anything special, but it was nice—white with dark-green trim, with Mamma's geraniums in pots on the front porch and Daddy's tomatoes growing in an old bathtub in the yard. From the front porch, the door opened right into the living room, where there was a sectional, and in front of it, the TV set. Along one wall was a mirrored cabinet where Mamma kept her collection of glass birds: seventeen of them, one for each year that she and Daddy had been married. Mamma dusted those birds all the time and, when we were little, wouldn't even let Danny and me go near them, that's how much she loved those birds. Anyway, that was the living room. Then there was a dining area, and then the kitchen. The bedrooms were at the back of the house. Mamma and Daddy had the biggest room, Grandma and Lila slept in the second biggest, and finally, in the very back, there was a little room for Danny and me. It was so narrow it barely fit our two beds, but it didn't bother me none, or at least not most of the time. Danny talked in his sleep sometimes, saying stupid things like "Fruitcake, where's the fruitcake?" Or this one time, he said, "Man, you *know* I don't want an elephant." But even that didn't bother me much, seeing as I was used to it and all. Finally, in a shed at the back of the house was a washing machine. On sunny days Grandma hung the washing out on a line and let the sun dry it. She said she didn't care that it was 1993, putting clean laundry in a machine to dry it was just plain stupid, especially in South Louisiana, where most days were sunny and hot.

All around the neighborhood were houses like ours, narrow and long, propped on blocks above the ground to keep them cool, with front porches and worn wooden floors. But one by one, the old neighbors were moving out. If new people didn't move in, the houses just sat there, getting lonelier and more dilapidated by the day.

When Gabriel Keyes and his little old auntie moved into an abandoned shotgun so small it looked like it had been built for midgets and so decrepit it looked like it could fall over, everything changed. Before Gabriel, I'd mainly been a loner, not because I didn't want friends, but more because I just didn't know how to get them. For one thing, I was massively uncoordinated, so the idea of going out for a pickup game of football or catch filled me with dread. I was skinny, undersized, nearsighted, and so pale that after an hour in the sun I'd be the color of a tomato. Mainly what I liked to do was read and play computer games, but seeing as we had one computer for all five of us and half the time Mamma wouldn't let me go near it, mainly what I did was read.

But there wasn't much time for reading, or much of anything else, once Gabriel Keyes came barging into my life, where he lodged himself as permanently as a brick. That was the year I was in fourth grade and he was in fifth. Even then, he was this huge kid, awkward and clumsy, with massive arms and legs, jiggling all over like he was filled with water balloons, and skin the color of apple juice. And could he *talk*. The thing with Gabriel was once he got going, there was no stopping him. And once he decided that you were his friend, you were his friend forever. That's how it was with him and me. It could be downright embarrassing to be seen with him, especially when he got to talking and wouldn't stop.

Truth was, and we all knew it, something was off about him, like maybe instead of a brain inside his head he had a busted hard drive. Kids said he was stupid, but that wasn't it. For one thing, even back in elementary school, he'd use all these big words—words like *pontificate* and *laparoscopic*. Also, when it came to numbers, he was like a walking calculator. But then he'd go and do the stupidest stuff, like when he wrote "I love you, Mrs. Rutlidge" on top of his social studies paper and had to be sent to the school counselor, or when he decided to stage an experiment to see if different colors weighed different amounts and poured a bunch of different colored paint out the second-floor art room window at school to see which color hit the ground first.

"That boy is one hundred percent stupid in the head," kids would say.

Me, I figured that Gabriel was like a big old dog, with his own kind of doggy-smartness and his tail either wagging or stuck between his legs. Anyway, like I was saying, one day Gabriel just kind of *appeared*, moving into that old house with its sagging roof and peeling paint. Before then, he'd been living some place in New Orleans, only Gabriel didn't say where or talk about why he'd moved or why he lived with his auntie instead of his parents.

I felt sorry for Gabriel, living the way he did, in that tiny little house with his tiny little auntie and no pets or even a single geranium in a single pot to cheer things up. But Gabriel didn't seem to mind.

"Home's where the heart's at, stupid," he said. "And anyway, it's just me and Auntie in our nuclear family unit. Plenty of room for us both."

"How are you related to your auntie?" I asked. "Because you sure don't look like her."

"We look alike inside," he said, pointing to his heart. "And that's the sworn one hundred percent truth of it."

Gabriel was only one grade ahead of me in school, but he looked like he was three years older. Kids at school used to make fun of him like crazy. But then, a year or so after he and his auntie moved in, he started to grow, until he was this huge kid, almost six feet tall and heavyset. When I was with him, I knew no one would ever mess with me. Even so, my mother didn't like him. She said he wasn't being raised properly, that every time she saw his auntie she looked like she'd been drinking. "You don't have to have a lot of money to live decent," Mamma said. "People always have a choice." But I didn't know how Mamma could tell whether Gabriel's auntie had been drinking, because the fact of the matter was that none of us ever saw her, not really. She worked nights, and when she was home, mainly what she did was sleep. Or at least that's what Gabriel would say. "Nah, man," he'd explain when I'd knock on his door to see if maybe we could hang at his house. "Not here—Auntie's sleeping. She needs to metabolically maximize. That means optimum slumber." Then he'd shut the door on me.

Lila, who was then in her senior year at Springs City High, had heard that Gabriel had seizures and that's why he was bad at school. Me, I didn't know one way or another why Gabriel was the way he was, why he either talked a mile a minute or acted like he didn't know how to speak English at all. But I did know that it had something to do with where Gabriel had been living *before* he and his auntie moved in at the end of the block and not something that had happened after, which was another thing folks said: "Fact of the matter is, that boy drank too much of his auntie's Budweiser, and it destroyed his brain cells, made him funny in the head," or "He got sick and had a high fever and his brain got infected, and when he got well again his mind was all scrambled." You heard different stories, but when I asked Gabriel himself, he just shrugged and said, "Folks like to talk, but I'm here now."

"There's just something about that boy," Mamma would say, over and over, but she could never tell me what exactly she didn't like about him except that he was a little older than me and talked too much. Even so, she was always inviting him over for dinner, and when he came she'd be sure to have plenty of extra food. That was Mamma. She loved to cook, and she looked like it too; I'm not saying she was fat, but she wasn't skinny either. It was more like she was round—round and strong, with a lap that was meant for sitting on. And Gabriel? He was always hungry. "Doesn't your auntie feed you, child?" Mamma would say, dishing out a second lamb chop or a helping of mashed potatoes or a piece of peach pie. But Gabriel would just shake his head up and down, licking his lips like a homeless mutt, and put his plate out for more. There was something downright annoying about him. He could drive you crazy, he ate like he'd never seen food before, but like I said, he was my best friend.

"What's this world coming to when a person doesn't take care of her own kin?" Mamma said after Gabriel had gone home one evening.

"The boy's all right. Leave him be," Daddy said.

"But that aunt of his. Why doesn't she feed him right?"

"She's just trying to get by like everyone else."

"I don't know, James. The whole damn neighborhood, it isn't what it used to be."

It was true. Old Mr. Samuels's house, in the middle of the block, looked like it would fall over in the next wind. Mr. Samuels—who spent most of his days on his front stoop in the sun, reading the sports section—didn't seem to notice. He was so old it was hard to tell if he even knew he was still alive. Then there was the house where two men covered top to bottom in tattoos lived. There were so many beer cans in their yard, it was like they were running a beer can farm.

Danny and Lila and I were under strict orders not to fool with them. And across from them was a brand-new family from some place in Africa. They barely came out at all, except to get inside their air-conditioned minivan, and didn't even stop to talk about the weather or say hello.

Other houses were little more than empty boxes surrounded by patches of weeds, an entire collection of old boards and broken windows, front porches that slanted down toward the sidewalk, and roofs that didn't keep the rain out. At night, when the wind whipped through those houses and the stray dogs began to howl, it was like the soundtrack of a horror movie—the one where the bad guy jumps out from behind the tree and starts slashing away at everyone. When it got stormy like that, even the birds freaked out; they'd be like *eep, eep, eeeeep,* flapping their wings around. There were stray dogs all over our neighborhood, little dirty dogs with square snouts and short, sharp teeth. I felt sorry for them, but they scared me too—especially late at night, when the wind howled along with them in a crazy chorus.

Other times, the street was so quiet that all you could hear was the mosquitoes eating away at the iron plants.

"When I was growing up, this block was so friendly," Mamma said. "Now I hardly know anyone."

"It's just the way of things," Daddy said. "There's no use trying to stop change."

"But I miss the way it used to be," Mamma said. "It was nice, being friends with all the neighbors."

She and Daddy were always saying things like that, going on and on about how our neighborhood used to be the kind of place where everyone knew everyone else—black, white, it didn't make no difference. Only now, with half the houses empty, people hid inside behind locked doors. Sometimes I'd overhear them talking about moving out to one of the nice new subdivisions on the far side of town where they were building a mall and solid brick houses with attached garages and all-new everything inside. But then Mamma would stop and say, "You know I'd love to move up there, James, but what about Mamma? She grew up on this very block, and she and my father raised me and my sister right here in this house. She likes it here."

"She'd like it there too."

"And what about church? If we moved, she wouldn't be able to walk to church."

"We'd drive her."

"You know it wouldn't be the same."

And on and on they'd talk like that, sometimes for hours, always going over the same points: new houses were expensive, and even though between the two of them they could afford one, their mortgage payments would eat up the money they were saving for Lila and me and Danny to go to college.

Lila said she didn't want their money, though. She said she wasn't going to go to college, that she had other plans. She and Mamma fought about it, with Mamma saying that no child of hers was going to throw her future away by working some dumb-ass dead-end job and didn't God give her brains so she could use them, and Lila saying that Mamma wasn't her mamma at all and to mind her own business and butt out.

"If I ain't your mamma, who is?" Mamma said during one of their blowups.

Lila sassed her with something like, "You may have fed me, but that doesn't mean you can control my *future*."

"Without a degree, you won't even have a future," Mamma mumbled. She herself had gone to beauty school. She'd wanted to be a makeup artist but ended up working at the Supercuts, making minimum plus tips. On a slow day she might come home with less in her pocket than she'd had when she'd started out in the morning. "No child of mine is going to make the same fool mistake," she said.

"Like I said," Lila retorted, "you're not my mother."

"And like I said, seeing that your real mother abandoned you and died, you don't got any choice."

"I've got as much choice as anyone," Lila said. "This is America."

"Go ahead, then, and ruin your life. You'll end up on the streets, and then you can do a stint in prison, a few rounds of rehab, and then back to the streets. Is that what you want?"

But that was nothing compared to the fight they had when Mamma found out that Lila was dating a thirty-year-old, someone named Zip. How she found out was that she snooped, getting into Lila's desk drawer, where she found all these photos of Lila and Zip. Mamma could see with just one glance that Zip wasn't a high school boy or even a college student, but a grown man, a man with wide shoulders and nice clothes and, from the looks of it, a car. That's when something in Mamma busted loose entirely, turning her into . . . into I don't know what . . . a screaming machine? Because for a while, that's all she did—scream. Mainly she screamed at Lila, calling her all kinds of bad things: an ingrate, a liar, a slut, a fool, an idiot, a loser, a hooker, a skank, and a selfish, spoiled brat.

"You want to end up pregnant and used, be my guest!" Mamma said.

"But he loves me!" Lila said. "He wants to marry me."

"Marry you? That's what he said?"

"As soon as I turn eighteen."

"And you believe him?"

"He loves me!"

"Jesus Christ! I didn't raise you to be a common slut!"

"Zip says I'm talented," Lila said. "He wants to help me launch my career."

"Your *career*?"

"I'm gonna be a singer."

"A singer? More like a stripper!"

"Mamma!"

"That man's nothing but a con, Lila. A con, pure and simple. And you're a damn fool if you believe one word he tells you."

The screaming would get to be so loud that the windows shook inside their frames, so loud that me and Danny would hide in our room with our hands over our ears, so loud that Grandma would beg them to quiet down. But no matter how many times Grandma calmed things down and made Mamma sit down with a glass of iced tea, it wouldn't last. She screamed at me. She screamed at Grandma. She even screamed at Danny, and he wasn't nothing but a little kid. The only one she didn't scream at was Daddy, probably because Daddy had a temper, and you didn't mess with him. He never hit anyone, but when he felt like he was cornered, all of a sudden—*boom!* His hands would ball into fists at his sides, his face would turn purple, he'd begin to shake, and then he'd blow up. I'd seen it only once or twice, but it was enough to make me know that I never did want to be on the receiving side of it, because once it started, the volcano inside him just kept spewing. No sir, you did *not* want to be anywhere near my father when he was angry.

Mainly, though, Daddy was a mild man, a mechanic who worked steady at Jerry Lane Trucking Services and came home tired, smelling like oil. He just loved vehicles. He loved everything about them: the way they purred when they were newly oiled, the way they smelled when they were new, the way a well-designed motor was like a work of art. Plus, he made a decent amount of money, meaning that he and Mamma could get a mortgage if they decided to move into the new subdivision. On the other hand, if they did that, they'd have to dip into our college funds . . . and back and forth and around and around they'd go, all their worries mixed up with Lila and then mixed up again with Grandma and then, in the final mix, with Danny and me.

Mamma would say, "I worry something awful about Grandma, the way she walks to church and back by herself all the time, and at all hours. I just wouldn't be able to forgive myself if someone harmed a hair on her head . . . but then again, her whole life is wrapped up in that church. All her friends are there, and it gives her something to do while we're at work and the children are at school. And I don't know, James, it would be nice for the boys to go to one of those new schools they got up at that end of the parish, and for Mamma to have her own room, because at her age—I don't need to be telling you this James—but at her age she ought to have a little privacy. I'm going to kill Lila, I swear to God, James, if that girl doesn't straighten up, and soon . . . what if she ends up dead in a ditch? Selling her body? Using? She's already drinking. Last week I smelled beer on her breath. She denied it, of course. But I know what I know, and I know that that girl is following in her mother's footsteps. And if she keeps going like she's going, Jesus . . . I don't even want to think about it. And I don't much like James Jr. hanging around all the time with that Gabriel character. And I know it's not his fault that he's the way he is . . ."

And on and on she'd go like that, Mamma doing most of the talking.

Then the day came when Lila, dressed in a short-short skirt with high heels and a pink blouse, told Mamma that she wasn't going to go to church anymore, not that day—it was a Sunday—and not any other day either. She announced that since she didn't believe in God she didn't see the point. "It's hypocritical," she said. "Not to mention boring."

"What do you mean you don't believe in God?"

"God is just a crutch for the masses," Lila said.

"Who taught you that? Zip?"

"Unlike you," Lila said, "I can actually think for myself."

"Seems to me that Zip is doing your thinking, not you."

"Seems to me that you're not even my mother," Lila said. "My real mother would understand."

That's when Mamma let loose and slapped her—smack!—across the face.

"Your so-called real mother was nothing but a whore at the end!" Mamma yelled. "And if you don't clean up your act, and fast, that's just where you're going too, young lady—six feet under. Is that what you want?"

But Lila didn't hear that part, because by then she'd run out of the house, slamming the door behind her.

"Go get her, James!" Mamma told Daddy. "Go bring her back."

But when Daddy took off after her, two things happened: The first was Lila had already disappeared down the block. The second was Daddy fell. We heard his body hitting the ground before we saw it. A second later, we'd followed him out to the sidewalk where he was lying on his side, gasping for air. "I . . . can't . . . breathe," he said.

"James! James! I'm here, baby, you're okay, baby," Mamma said as Grandma called 911. But by the time the ambulance came, he was dead. Heart attack is what they told us. And just like that, he was gone.

2

THEN CAME SAD

Looking back, none of us could say exactly what happened, only that Lila must not have known about Daddy, because if she had known about Daddy, then surely she would have come straight home. But not only did she not come straight home, she didn't come home *at all*. It just about busted Mamma up, burying Daddy while Lila was who-knew-where. She blamed herself for Daddy's death, too, saying that if she hadn't made him go get Lila he wouldn't have died. When Grandma told her that it was God's will, that Daddy had died because his heart had given out, plain and simple, Mamma went on, saying that if she hadn't ridden Lila so hard, not only would Lila not have run out like she did, but all five of us would still be together, safe and sound.

It was too late to bring Daddy back—he was sleeping forever in the shade of a live oak tree at Crystal Springs

Memorial—but it wasn't too late to find Lila. After Daddy's funeral, Mamma put pretty much all she had into tracking Lila down in order to bring her home, where she belonged. When she wasn't at work, Mamma was on the phone, talking to the police, to the sheriff's office, even to the FBI. When she wasn't on the phone, she was stomping all over South Louisiana, trying to find someone who could help her. She even hired a private investigator. After all, she said, how hard could it be to find a seventeen-year-old redhead with no money, no car, no credit cards, and no sense? The only thing Lila had taken with her when she ran from the house was her driver's license. How do you track down a driver's license? Still and all, Mamma thought that if Lila had gone and run off with Zip, then at least the police wouldn't just brush Mamma's worries aside, saying that kids ran away every day of the week and most of the time they showed up when they were good and ready, but in any case once they crossed state lines there wasn't much they could do about it and so forth and so on. As best as I can make out, there were all kinds of legal technicalities and complications, even though from Mamma's point of view, there was nothing complicated about it: Lila had run off with some thug who went by the name of Zip, which, given that Lila was only seventeen, amounted to kidnapping or worse.

And then the day came when Lila turned eighteen. A week later, a letter arrived.

Dear Mamma and Daddy,

I'm sorry I ran off without even saying goodbye, or telling you anything, or calling. But I just couldn't stand living with you anymore, all the fighting, and all the terrible things Mamma said about me. For your information, Zip and I have gotten married. He loves me, and I love him. Also, we have left Louisiana and are heading to California, where Zip knows people in the entertainment industry and I'm going to try to break into the music business. Don't worry, we'll both get jobs. I'll let you know when we get to California, but don't try to track me down. I've changed my name.

Lila

So Grandma got her privacy after all, and we all settled into a life of sadness. Mamma drooped under her sadness. When she came home from work, all she could do was plop herself down in front of the TV and have herself a Coke. "That child is going to give me a heart attack, too, sure enough," Mamma would say with tears in her eyes. "I just pray she knows what she's doing. I just pray dear God Jesus will look after her."

"At least she's gone and gotten herself legally married," Grandma pointed out.

"Legally married!" Mamma cried. "If it's so *legal*, then why didn't Lila go on down to the church and get married properly? Why didn't she bring Zip by to meet her family? What's she running away from?"

"How do you know she didn't get married in a church?" Grandma said, but Mamma held her ground, arguing that no seventeen-year-old sneaks off and gets married without anyone even knowing about it unless she had to, and quick. "I sure hope she's not pregnant. I sure hope this Zip isn't just using her. Help me, Lord . . ." Mamma cried so much her eyes were permanently swollen.

"I ran her out of the house," Mamma said to Grandma. "If anything happens to her, it's because of me."

"You did the best you could," Grandma said, patting Mamma's hand like Mamma was a little girl. "That's all we can do. Lord knows, I'm not sure anything I could have done, back then, would have helped your sister . . ."

And then the two of them, mother and daughter, would just sit there, talking about Lila and looking sad.

I was still pretty young, so it was hard for me to understand all the ins and outs of what Lila had done. But the truth is that after a while, Lila began to fade from my memory. I just couldn't remember all that much about her. And as for Danny, he barely remembered her at all. I remembered her flaming red hair and how she liked nothing better than painting her fingernails and the deep, husky, throaty sound of her voice, but it was hard for me to keep her in my head. And later, when Grandma took sick with cancer and lost all her hair from the treatment they gave her, I stopped thinking about Lila completely. Finally, Grandma said that she'd had enough, she was an old lady, and she was ready to go to God. After Grandma passed, it was just Danny, Mamma, me, and the birds left in that old house in Crystal Springs, and suddenly the house seemed as big as an art museum.

The year Grandma died was the same year that Danny was fixing to move from elementary up to middle school, and even though I still looked like I was nine, I was moving to high school. For a little while, the house had filled up with Mamma's friends from church and people she knew from work, but then they stopped coming. Bit by bit, even when they called, Mamma wouldn't want to be talking to them at all. "Tell her I'm not home, James Jr.," she'd say, or "Tell them I'll call tomorrow." Only she never did call tomorrow. More and more, when the phone rang, Mamma wouldn't even let *us* answer it. "Let it ring," she'd say. "If it's important, they'll call back." She shut the curtains, keeping them closed even during the day. And if someone came by, say with a pie or a baked ham, she'd pretend we weren't home. Then she unplugged the phone answering machine, saying that her heart was just too heavy to sit on the phone *talking*. Meantime, I'd moved into Grandma's and Lila's old room, and the house seemed to stretch from one side of the world to the next, with nothing but empty spaces in between. Bit by bit, folks stopped coming by, and the phone, when it did ring, rang into silence. Even the birds noticed. Instead of singing—*tweet tweet tweet*—all day long, they'd sit around, not talking at all, or if they did talk, they'd say sad things, like *I miss my baby! I miss my baby!* This one time, when I got home from school, they took one look at me and said, *Help me, Lord!*

I can't blame Mamma, neither, because she did her best, going out to work every day and making sure that Danny and I had the right uniforms and the right pens and pencils and that we did all our homework and what all that we were supposed to be doing. But even I could tell that things weren't right with her no more. Something was wrong, so wrong that it was almost as if something busted deep within, a spring or something, and once that spring broke, there was no fixing it. Every night she'd grumble about how the laundry machine was so old it was going to break and the plumbing didn't work too good either and without Daddy how was she going to keep the place up? Sometimes her eyes would well with tears. Then she'd sniff them back inside her eyeballs, stretch out her hands to both of us, and say, "I'm sorry, boys. We'll get by. You'll see. We've got each other. Your dad and your grandmother are in heaven, watching over us. God is good."

Sonny and Cher just stood there on their perches, staring out through the bars of their cage, and occasionally looking up to say, *Jesus! Grandma! Jesus!*

God may have been good, but Mamma was getting worse. All day long, she muttered to herself and drank orange soda and Coke like her life depended on it. But no matter how much she drank, she said she was thirsty, that the heat was killing her, and she kept getting skinnier and skinnier. Summer came, and I'd hear her in her room drinking orange soda and praying to Jesus and talking to Daddy and to Grandma and to anyone else who might be listening, I reckon. Her words would all be running together, like the runny yellow part of a fried egg, and I could tell she was crying, too, because it was like there was a fist all balled up in her throat and she had to squeeze it to get the words out. She worried so much about money that she sold our computer—it didn't fetch much, she said, but it would help—and got so skinny that her wedding band started sliding off her finger. She put it in her jewelry box so she wouldn't lose it. Finally, she got so skinny that she went to the doctor.

"Guess what, boys?" she said that night at dinner. "Doctor told me that I had *stress*. As if I didn't know. What do you think I'd have, losing your father, and then my baby girl, and then Grandma, one after another, and I'm not yet forty years old! What did he think I had? Measles? Pass the butter, please."

When that old washing machine of ours finally broke for real, Mamma sat down on the sofa and cried like a baby. But she picked herself up again, carting our dirty things to the Supercuts where she worked, where they had a washing machine for doing the towels, and things returned to normal. The new school year up and started again, with Danny in seventh grade and me in tenth. Mamma kept right on drinking orange soda and cutting hair—doing lots of overtime, too, because the pay was better—until one day in late September, just after Danny turned twelve. That was the day that I got home from school to find Mamma in her bed with the door closed and the shades drawn. Only she wasn't breathing anymore, and that's because she was dead.

Even before I came tiptoeing in the way I always did when she worked overtime, I knew she was dead. I knew it before my brain knew it. So it wasn't like I was *thinking* that maybe she was dead, I just *knew* it, the way you know when a storm is coming on. I could feel it, like stillness in the room—only the stillness was cold, so cold that, even though it was hot outside and the air-conditioning unit in Mamma's window wasn't working so well, I felt like my bones had turned to ice. She was laying on her side, with the quilt pulled up over her shoulder, and her eyes were closed, like she was sleeping. Only when I put my hand up over her mouth, no breath came out, which was when I knew for the second time—this time in my *mind*— that she was dead, and I began to scream.

I don't know how long I stood there screaming, but I do know that after a while my throat began to hurt something awful. I went into the kitchen to get a glass of water and to call someone, but when I went to pick up the phone, my mind just froze up on me. I couldn't think of a single person to call. I guess I could have gone over to one of the neighbors' houses or called one of Mamma's friends from work or the minister at church or even called the police or 911 or the school principal, but my mind wasn't clear and the only person in the whole world I could think of calling was Gabriel.

"What do you mean your mamma's dead?" he said.

"I mean she's dead," I said. "Dead and not breathing. And she's lying up in her bed like that, and Danny's going to be coming home on the school bus any minute now, and if he sees her like that, oh Lord . . . poor Mamma, poor Danny . . ."

"We gotta contemplate," Gabriel said. Then he said, "Hold on. I'm on my way." Being that Gabriel didn't live but half a block from our house, it wasn't more than a minute until he was standing with me in Mamma's bedroom, looking down at her, while the air-conditioning unit in the window went *thump-thump-thump.*

"This is reprehensible and terribly awful," he said.

"Yeah."

"Your daddy gone too." As if I didn't know that. But truthfully, I didn't really know anything right then. It was like a bad dream, the worst dream you could ever imagine, with me and Gabriel standing over Mamma, and Mamma not moving or talking or breathing or doing *nothing,* and Danny on his way home. Meanwhile, I was just a kid myself—just fifteen, and Gabriel sixteen, and Danny twelve, still sleeping with his favorite stuffed animal, Bow-Wow, and insisting that it was a dog, even though anyone with two eyes could see that Bow-Wow was a beat-up old teddy bear with fur the color of oatmeal and only one ear.

3

HOW IT STARTED

"Mamma's dead," I repeated.

"Undeniably factual."

"Mamma! That's my mamma!"

"It's bad, all right."

"What we gonna do?"

"It's okay," Gabriel said.

Suddenly, I was furious. I turned from Mamma, and looking at Gabriel, began to scream, "What you mean? Okay? It's not okay, Gabriel. That's my mother! And she's dead!" I tore at Mamma's covers, threw her alarm clock against the wall, and then started kicking Gabriel in the shins, kicking as hard as I could. But before I knew it, Gabriel had picked me clear up and off my feet, hugging me so hard that I could barely breathe. When he put me down again, I was calmer.

"I know it's bad," Gabriel said, bending over to examine his legs.

"Did I hurt you?" I said, suddenly remorseful for what I'd done.

"Don't worry about it," he said. "Because the thing is, I'm going to help you. I'm going to assist you in all manner and potential. Because you're in trouble, deep. I make this solemn promise, right here, right now, that I'm going to help you."

"How you going to help me?" I said, fury welling up in me again. But this time I was too tired to do much of anything, and so I just sat there, my whole body shaking while the tears and snot fell onto my lap and backed up into my throat and I got all covered with my own slime.

"What we've got to do," Gabriel said, stopping to scratch the back of his neck, "is . . ."

"Is what?" I said. Truthfully, I didn't think he was going to say anything at all other than a whole lot of *blah blah blah* like usual.

But Gabriel surprised me. He bit his lower lip, then his upper. "What we've got to do is, we've got to take your mother and put her somewhere where no one's gonna find her, not ever, okay? Someplace of utmost security and secrecy, beyond speculating about. Because if they find out about your mamma passing like that, oh brother . . ." Shaking his head, Gabriel let his words trail off.

"What you mean?"

"Boy, don't you know anything?"

"Mamma's dead" was all I could say. "I've got to call someone. I've got to call the police."

"Don't do that."

"Got to. Or I'll call our pastor is what I'll do."

Gabriel took my hand, squeezing it so hard it hurt. "You can't communicate this to no one."

I began to cry again, gushing tears like my entire body was made out of tears, gushing so many tears that I could feel them falling down my neck and my chest.

"You can't do no calling at all," Gabriel said. "Because if the police or your pastor find out about you—they find out you and Danny don't have no parents no more—first thing they're going to do is come on over here and take the two of you away and put you someplace terrible and make you live with people who'll beat you just because you're breathing. Because if they can't find no kin to you—you got any other family you know about?"

I shook my head. There hadn't been many of us to begin with, seeing as Mamma had only her one sister, and Daddy didn't have any brothers and sisters at all except for a much older half brother who'd been killed in Vietnam. So the truth is, except for Lila, they'd all done died, and now it was just Danny and me.

"Because if you don't have kin, they just ship you any old anywhere, and then you and Danny, see, you're on your own. You'll be lucky if they give you any food at all, because when kids don't have parents, see, that's how it was for me before my auntie found me and we moved up here to Crystal Springs. Because back before—well, it's not like I remember it so good in New Orleans, but wasn't nothing *good* about it. Foster care. That's what it is. They told me that I was going to be living in foster care, and when I heard that, I was prognosticating that I'm going to go live with Mr. and Mrs. Foster—that's how little I was when my mother and father got the virus and died. I don't even right remember them. And I'm thinking I'm going to live in some nice, fine house with Mr. and Mrs. Foster, but instead they go put me with Mrs. Evil. That woman was so mean alligators were scared of her. And well, all's I'm saying is that even though you're already pretty big in the eyes of the authorities, you're still a minor citizen and ward of the state. You don't want to be going to no foster care, no way. I know. So this is what we got to do . . ."

But I wasn't much following what he was saying. Virus? Foster care? *Prognosticating?* What did that have to do with me and Danny? And with my mother? When I began to think about her again, I couldn't help myself, because next thing I know I'm yelling out for her, yelling "Mamma, Mamma!" like a baby. But the more I yelled out her name, the deader she got. How could Mamma just go and not be there no more? It didn't make sense. It didn't make sense at all.

Neither did Gabriel. He was yapping away like a dog does when he knows something you don't know, like maybe there's lightning coming or a snake in the grass, but he can't tell you about it except by barking and growling and pulling at the leash. Even with me crying and shaking, and with all the snot and tears flying out of me, Gabriel wouldn't let up. He said that if people knew that Mamma had died and that there weren't any other grown-ups in the house, and there wasn't anyone else who was blood kin to us in Louisiana—leastways no one we knew about, not even a half cousin or a great-aunt or no one—well, then, someone from the mayor's office or maybe from the police would come and get us and make us live somewhere where we didn't know anyone and where they wouldn't give us enough food and would maybe lock us up and not let us use the toilet, and I'd never see Danny again.

"What time you got?" Gabriel said after I'd finally calmed down some.

"Three."

"Three already?"

"Danny's fixing to come home soon."

"Here's what we'll do," Gabriel said. He pulled me into his big old meat-paws with such force that my face mushed up against his chest and I could hear his heart beating. Then he told me.

Now, if I'd been in my right mind, I might not have gone along with Gabriel's plan, but seeing that I wasn't in my right mind, I did. And truthfully, even if I had been in my right mind, I didn't see what else I *could* do. Plus, Gabriel was like an eighteen-wheeler with worn-out pads: once he started on down the hill, no amount of hitting the brakes was going to stop him.

He said that, first off, I had to keep Danny away from Mamma's bedroom no matter what, that I had to tell him that she was sick with something bad that we could catch and that she'd given me money to take him out to the Piccadilly for dinner. Seeing that Mamma kept some money in a coffee can in the kitchen and more in her wallet, getting the money was no problem. And because Danny was just a little kid who thought going anywhere was a big adventure, I didn't have to do any convincing to get him to go with me to the Piccadilly. He ordered the Dilly special: two pieces of fried chicken plus two vegetables plus a roll plus dessert. I wasn't hungry. Gabriel said to keep him at the Piccadilly for as long as possible, which wasn't all that hard, given how much he had ordered. Then, when we got home, I had to make sure that he got good and in bed and not let him anywhere near Mamma's room no matter what. That was the hardest part because Danny was only twelve, scrawny and bony, with enormous dark eyes, ears that stuck straight out, and mud-brown hair that was so short and so thick it looked like bristles. He wanted to tell Mamma about something he'd done at school and then he wanted to show her the A he'd gotten on his math test and then he wanted her to give him a good-night kiss and then he said that he had a stomachache and wanted Mamma to give him something for it because he thought he was going to throw up. Meanwhile, all I wanted to do was sit on the floor and cry like a baby, but Gabriel said I had to pretend like everything was normal. So I told Danny that his stomachache would go away all by itself if he lay down and went to sleep.

"I'm going to be sick," he said.

"You just ate too much, is all."

"Mamma always gives me that pink medicine—the one that tastes like chocolate and peppermint."

"I'll get it for you."

"What if you give me the wrong kind?"

I went and got the medicine, but he kept complaining about how much his stomach hurt and how he needed Mamma to come and sit with him and rub his stomach until he felt better.

"Just shut up and go to sleep."

"You're not my boss. Why can't I see Mamma?"

"She told me special that if you went in there she'd kill you good and dead."

"She did not."

"She told me not to let you in, boy, and if I do let you in she's going to punish both of us. She meant it too. She was using her mean voice."

I felt bad talking about my mother that way, but once I got going, I could barely stop myself. The lies came so easily to me it was like I was living in a movie and just saying my lines, nice and natural, the way I was supposed to. But I felt sick doing it, sick knowing that Mamma was dead and we'd never see her no more, and just plain sick. It didn't help that Cher and Sonny kept hopping around their cage and saying, *Lord have mercy!* But bit by bit I managed to calm Danny down. And then I told him that if he'd just shut up and stopped whining he could stay up and watch TV with me. He went to get Bow-Wow, and then we sat down to watch a dumb show about doctors. By the time the first commercials were coming on he was getting sleepy. I made him go to bed, saying that if he didn't I'd tell Mamma about it in the morning and he'd be in trouble.

I made sure that Danny was good and asleep, with his mouth dribbling drool on his pillow and his hands stroking the sheet back and forth, like he sometimes does when he's dreaming, and then I called Gabriel.

4

WHERE WE PUT HER

Gabriel came over. His auntie worked nights, so it was easy for him to get out like that. First we made sure that Danny was still sound asleep, hugging his stuffed teddy bear dog and breathing deeply. Then he and I went into Mamma's room, wrapped her up in the quilt, carried her clear out the front door, and took her around the corner and down a block or two. There wasn't nothing to it; Mamma had shrunk down so much it was like carrying a child, and like I said, Gabriel was big. He took her shoulders and head, and I had her feet. Under the quilt I could feel her toes and her ankles, her bones and her knees. I could even feel her nightgown, swishing around over her skin. "Mamma . . . Mamma," I kept saying, and then I'd begin to sniffle and choke on my snot, but Gabriel hushed me up. Finally, arriving on a block where most of the houses looked bedraggled and empty, we stopped and looked around.

"This one's good," he said, stopping in front of an old sagging shotgun shack. Its front porch was half-on and half-off, tilting like it was about to slide into the street, and the front door had been spray-painted with graffiti. "No one's going to be poking around here looking for a corpse." He was right. With all the weeds and broken glass everywhere, the McDonald's wrappers, soda cans, torn-up newspapers, and old shoes, it was a dump. The house was raised up on concrete blocks, so there was plenty of room underneath. Gabriel and I got down on our knees and put Mamma in front of us on the ground. "Ready?" Gabriel said. I nodded, and the two of us pushed her under the house.

Then we heard light footsteps. When we looked behind us, we saw a dog. It had pointy ears and mangy brown fur, and it came right up to us sniffing in the air before it lowered its nose right where we'd shoved Mamma. "Get on away out of here!" Gabriel said, getting up and waving his arms. When the dog didn't move, Gabriel picked up a board and, waving it over his head, chased it away.

"No mongrel hound is going to bother your mamma none, boy," he said. "I chased that dog away good and for real."

"What if it comes back?"

"I'll kill it, it tries to come back. But it won't," he said as he crouched down again next to me. Together we rolled Mamma all the way under the house, and then, when we couldn't get her any farther, we got onto our backs and pushed her with our feet. I hated doing that—pushing her with my feet like she was an old rug, putting her under the house with the rats and the empty beer bottles and the old wiring and the whatever else that might be down there—but we had to do what we had to do, and between the two of us, we hid her completely.

"One more item we must consider enacting on the agenda," Gabriel said. The next thing I knew, he'd gone into the house itself, walking right in through the busted-up front door, and was hauling out all kinds of junk—old boards and a busted-up microwave and some packing cases and bundles of old wire. Bit by bit he packed all that stuff under the house. Finally he carried out a mattress that he found in there and shoved that under the house, too, saying, "No stray dog going to be bothering her none, not now, not with all this stuff all around her." He crossed his arms over his chest with a look of satisfaction, like he'd just washed his car or finished painting a room.

"That's that, I guess," he said.

That's when I started throwing up. I threw up and threw up. I threw up even after there wasn't anything left to throw up but spit.

When I was done, when there was nothing left to get out, Gabriel put his arm around my shoulder. "I know it's bad," he said. "It's as bad as bad can be. But you're not alone. You aren't in isolation or sequestration. You've still got your brother. And you've got me. And I will never, not ever, leave you. Hear?" Then he led me up to the sagging old front porch and got down on his knees. "Holy Jesus, have pity on this here orphan boy, James, and take his mother up to heaven to be in your heavenly arms, amen," he said.

"Amen," I said.

"Only thing is," Gabriel said, "you can't never, and I mean never *ever*, tell Danny where we done put her. You do that, and next thing you know, every policeman in the city is going to be pounding on your door. Then it's all over. By the time they're done with you, you'll be shipped off to prison. Danny will land in JV. Because Danny? He'll lead them right to this very spot."

Then Gabriel walked me back home and told me to get some sleep. As if I could sleep. As if I could do anything at all but shake, like my whole body was vomiting and it would never stop. But there was nothing else to do. I got undressed and got in bed in the middle room—the one that used to be Lila and Grandma's, and then just Grandma's—and just lay there, not sleeping. All I could think of was Mamma, the way her body wasn't very heavy and how I could feel her bones through the quilt we'd wrapped her in. I thought about the dog with the pointy ears. I thought about how, even if no dogs bothered her, the cockroaches and the rats would eat her for breakfast, lunch, and dinner. By the time I'd gotten into bed, I had to slam my fist in my mouth to keep from screaming. Then I thought about how stupid I was to listen to Gabriel, how Danny would feel when he found out that Mamma was dead, and how, at any moment, the police would come knocking on the door to haul my ass off to prison, even without Danny knowing about what we'd done.

Sure enough, I heard a siren in the distance. I was so scared that I almost peed on myself. But then the noise passed, and everything was quiet again. Everything, that is, but the sound of a dog barking in the distance and the whooshing wheeze of my own breath. My breathing came out sharp and hoarse and raggedy all at once: *haaagh, haaaaghh.* I sounded like a werewolf.

I tried to read—I was reading *To Kill a Mockingbird* for school, which was pretty good—but that didn't work either. All I could think of was Mamma. All I could do was cry.

Finally, after not sleeping for an hour or two, I went into Mamma's room and opened up her jewelry box. When you opened it, it played a little tinkling kind of song. The inside was lined with white silk. I held up her heart necklace—the one she always said reminded her of how much she loved her kids—and then I put her wedding ring on my finger. I don't know why I was doing like that, I just was. When I was done, I put all her jewelry back, closed the lid, and put the case in her top drawer. Finally I tiptoed into my old room, the one that Danny and I had shared up until the time that Grandma died. My old bed was still jammed up in there, and I crawled under the covers. Next to me, Danny was sleeping like he always slept, all curled up into this weird position, with one arm thrown over his face and Bow-Wow upside down under his elbow. At least he wasn't talking in his sleep. I watched his mouth twitching back and forth like he wanted to say something, and now and then he'd gulp air and groan, but then he'd roll over and start twitching and sighing all over again, tumbling around in his dreams.

I never did know Lila that well. She was eight years older than me, for one thing, and for another, like I already said, she wasn't really my sister. She was my cousin. Mamma and Daddy took Lila in when Lila was just a baby herself. Seven years later they had me, and after that, along comes Danny.

But to tell you the truth, I never did think about her that much one way or the other. She was just there, like the furniture or the sky. After Mamma died, the only thing I really remembered about Lila was how much she and Mamma used to fight. Next thing we knew, she'd gone off with Zip, heading for California.

Truthfully, I hadn't given much thought to her. When Daddy died, I was sad enough as it was without spending my time worrying about my sister who was really my cousin. But after Mamma died? Then all I did was think about Lila, wondering where she'd gone to and if she'd ever come back. It started that very night. I wanted Lila to come home so badly that I almost convinced myself that if only I wished for her hard enough, she'd be back in no time.

First thing in the morning, Danny woke up and figured out that things weren't right. How I knew is that I didn't sleep at all that night, and then, suddenly, I did. I must have been sleeping deeply too—the kind of sleep where you're so tired that you don't even dream—because the next thing I knew, Danny was swatting me on the shoulder and saying, "Get out of my room, James. This my room now. You've got your own room. What are you doing in here?" and on and on like that, like I was some alien space-age creature who'd come to take him away in my spaceship.

"Huh?" I said. "What?"

"Get on outta here," he said. "Pee-ew! You're disgusting. Your breath smells so bad it could kill an entire city."

Rubbing sleep out of my eyes, I blinked awake, remembering everything that had happened. I half expected to hear a pounding at the door or a siren or, at the very least, the phone ringing, but instead all I heard was the usual not-much-of-anything: Birds twittering in the yard. A truck rumbling past somewhere. Wind. I got up and looked around. I even poked my head out the door. Nothing—or rather, nothing other than the usual scene. Half-dead houses, half-dead trees, and half-dead weeds wilting in the Louisiana heat.

I love you! I love you! Sonny and Cher sang when I went past.

Danny got up and went to the bathroom. I could hear him in there, brushing his teeth. After he finished, he went and put on his school uniform and then went into the kitchen and fixed himself a bowl of cereal. When he was done eating, he got up again and went straight for Mamma's door.

"Don't go in there."

"What's your problem? I'm just gonna tell Mamma that I'm going to school, like I always do."

"No."

"What you mean 'no'? Mamma?" he said, knocking on the door.

"See?" I said after a moment or two elapsed. "She's sick, and don't want to be bothered."

"Mamma?" he said again, real softly this time, as if maybe he'd figured out that Mamma had died and while he was sleeping Gabriel and I had gone and put her body under an abandoned shotgun on Twenty-Third Street.

"You're gonna miss your bus." He took one more look at me, looking me in the face like maybe he'd seen me before, but maybe not, and finally scurried on out the door. Leaving me alone with nothing to do but wait. What was I going to tell Danny?

5

THE WAY IT WAS
WITH GABRIEL

Maybe it was just because he was so big and bulky, with a slow-motion way of moving, that people thought something was wrong with him. But Gabriel wasn't some kind of freak. He was just slow. He walked slow, like an old man, with a lumbering, back-and-forth gait. He talked slow, too, and now and again, when he was nervous, he'd mumble or stutter, making it hard to understand him. When he thought, it was almost as if you could watch him thinking, seeing how one thought would follow the next, inside his brain. His smile was slow, his hands were slow, even his breathing was slow. The only time he sped up was when he caught hold of an idea, or rather, when an idea caught hold of *him*. Then there was no talking to him, no reasoning, no resisting. He was like a slow-moving storm that way, so big and so powerful that something as thin and skitter-scatter as words couldn't even begin to change the course of his lumbering momentum. Long vocabulary words would spew out of him like lava, endlessly long words that erupted, as if from an overheated belly, as if from a fire so hot it burned him up, sending a cascade of the kinds of words they test you on into the air. It wasn't just the big words he knew. When it came to numbers, he was amazing, a certified brainiac. The real truth is he didn't seem smart at all, and he wasn't, not in the usual ways. It was almost like half his brain was made of computer chips and the other half was made of bricks.

Also, he was sweet, always wanting to help out and take care of you and be your friend. But even that could be embarrassing. Like this one time, in ninth grade. I had just started out at Springs City High, all new kids from all over, plus suddenly we didn't just go to two or three classrooms but had lots of different classes to take, all in separate wings and floors. Between classes, the halls were so crowded that half the time I wasn't even sure I was heading in the right direction. But at least the freshmen were kept a little bit separate, with most of our classes in the freshmen annex, which wasn't much more than a wing that jutted back behind the rest of the school. Even so, it meant that for the second year in a row I wasn't going to have to worry much about Gabriel, about how awkward he could be.

Wrong. One day, I wasn't doing much of anything, just talking to some guys I'd met whose lockers were near mine. I began to think that maybe there was hope for me, that maybe

I could make some new friends, friends who were normal, and maybe even be invited to parties or to hang out. They seemed like pretty nice guys, cool, like they had some secret knowledge that no one else had yet. But just as we were getting into it, talking about stupid stuff—LSU football, pretty girls—who comes sauntering around the corner but good old Gabriel, more than six feet tall, slow as a turtle, and wearing an LSU Tigers T-shirt that must have been at least two sizes too small. His glasses were falling down his nose, his face was shiny with sweat, and the laces on his basketball shoes were untied and flopping. He looked like the Pillsbury Doughboy, only with spiky black hair. His forehead sprouted acne. His zipper was only half-zipped.

"MY MAN JAMES!" He didn't say it. He bellowed it. He mooed it. He was as loud as a whole pack of animals. He came over, put his arm around me. "HOW'S MY HOMEBOY DOING NOW YOU'RE IN HIGH SCHOOL, JAMES?"

It didn't take but two seconds for my new friends to give each other sideways glances and melt away into the hallway. And meantime, I'm thinking I'm going to have to lose Gabriel, because friendship or no friendship, hanging out with the kid was just too embarrassing—particularly as I myself wasn't exactly what you'd call at the top of the popularity mountain. Actually, I wasn't even halfway up the slope. Truth? Small for my age, with tortoise-shell glasses that I used for reading and knobby knees like a giraffe's, I was at the very bottom, hovering just over the total rejects and nerds who did things like pick their nose in class, or who smelled, or who cried whenever anyone said anything mean to them. All I needed was Gabriel around to sink me entirely.

Except that being associated with Gabriel had its upside, too, its own kind of cool. Girls would come up to me and say, "You know that big dude?" When I told them Gabriel was my neighbor and that he'd lived somewhere in New Orleans before coming up to Crystal Springs, they'd look at me with a new kind of respect, like maybe, even though Gabriel was goofy, I was somehow hanging with the *man*. Or if I went somewhere with him, a store or the KFC or whatever, people would look and see the two of us together, and then they'd pay attention to me. Sometimes people would say things to me like "He your big brother or your bodyguard?" or say things to Gabriel like "Yo, dog, you be good," and I'd feel like I was somebody.

I guess you could say that, even though he was my best friend and I was his, there was a lot of love-hate going on, too, at least on my side. On his, there was nothing I could say or do that would put me in the wrong.

"What are you doing hanging around with that idiot boy?" Lila used to say. "That boy's soft in the head." But of course that was before, when we were still a family.

But no matter what, with Gabriel, you always knew where you stood. If you were his friend, you were his friend for life. He'd tell you things that didn't seem to make much sense. For example, he mentioned that he knew the measure of angles even before he'd measured them, that he could feel colors, and that trees talked in their own secret language that wasn't like human language. He told me once that he wasn't quite sure how his auntie was his auntie, but that she'd rescued him. Rescued him? I didn't know what that meant. All I knew was that I sure wished his auntie would come over and rescue me.

On the day after we put Mamma under the house, I half expected that, as soon as Danny was out the door, she'd show up. But of course she didn't. She hardly ever showed her face at all. It was almost like she was hiding something—like maybe *she'd* put someone's body under a house and didn't want anyone to find out. As for Gabriel? I waited for him to knock on the door like he sometimes did so we could walk to school together, but he didn't come by.

Once I got Danny out of the house, I didn't know what to do with myself. I just knew that I wasn't going to go to school that day. I sat around for a while, not doing much of anything. I cried. I took Mamma's jewelry box out again and opened it, but after two or three notes of its tinkling music, I closed it up. Then I made Mamma's bed. I don't know why. I just thought it might be something she'd want me to do. I made my bed. I made Danny's bed. I went into the kitchen and opened the refrigerator door, but I wasn't hungry. I washed out Danny's cereal bowl and put it up in the dish drainer. Then I washed his spoon.

I went outside. The sun was already hot, and even though it was getting on toward October, you could tell it was going to be one of those heavy gray days that make you feel like maybe you got cotton stuffed down your throat, because that's how hot it is. Like you can't breathe. I looked up and down the street to see if maybe the police were coming, but aside from a couple cars passing by, the street was as quiet as quiet can be.

I walked down the block to Gabriel's house and knocked on the door, hoping that, like me, he was afraid to go to school and had holed up at home. By and by, I heard footsteps. But it wasn't Gabriel who opened the door; it was his tiny little auntie. Truthfully, I was shocked to see her. Most times, when I went to Gabriel's house—which really wasn't very often—she was either at work or sleeping. Now she stood in the doorway in front of me, wearing a ratty pink bathrobe and staring at me with bright eyes. She wasn't drinking or anything like that. She just seemed bewildered, like she'd forgotten who I was.

"What do you want, James?" she finally said, rubbing her eyes. "Aren't you supposed to be in school? Is something wrong? Why you looking at me that way?"

"I'm sorry to disturb you, ma'am," I said. "But I was thinking. Is Gabriel here?"

"He better not be," Gabriel's auntie said. She was as skinny and tiny as Gabriel was big and heavy, with bones no bigger than a chicken's. It was like they'd come from two different species entirely. How the two of them were kin was a mystery, but I wasn't much thinking about that now. "What's wrong with you?" she added. "You look like you've seen a ghost."

"No, ma'am," I said.

"No, ma'am, you haven't seen a ghost, or no, ma'am, you don't *want* to see no ghost?" When I didn't answer but just stood there, she said, "Never mind, James. I'm just messing with you. But you look downright peaked. You feel all right? You want me to fetch you a cold drink or a glass of juice?"

"No, ma'am," I said again.

"All right then," she said. "You better go on down to school. I know your mamma doesn't want to hear that you've been playing hooky."

Finally, when it looked like Gabriel's auntie didn't have much more to say, I walked back to our end of the street, went back inside the house, sat down on Mamma's living room set, and cried. Then I fell asleep. I don't know how long I slept, but when I woke up, the birds were saying, *Get up! Sun's up! Rise and shine!* It was afternoon. Danny was standing over me wearing his school uniform, his booksack on his back.

"Where's Mamma?" he said.

6

TELLING DANNY

I told him. Except for the part about where we buried her, I blurted out the whole story.

Even before I was finished, he started screaming. "You liar! You liar! You liar!" Then he went into Mamma's room, calling her name, looking under the bed, in her closet. He pulled all her clothes out—dresses, shoes—throwing them onto the floor, as if maybe Mamma were hiding, and if only he looked hard enough, he'd find her. When he couldn't, he began to throw things; bottles of perfume, magazines, pillows, handbags, and hairbrushes all went flying through the air. "You liar! I hate you!" he said, coming out of Mamma's room with his face covered in tears and his fists balled up into hard little rocks. A moment later, he was pummeling me with those fists, hitting me everywhere—in my stomach, in my face. I put up my hands to defend myself, but then he started kicking me too. He kicked me, wham, in the shin, and then his teeth were in me, sinking into my hand. That's when

I punched him one, good, in the stomach. He landed with a thud at my feet.

"Liar," he screamed. "I hate you! I hate you! I hate you!"

As his screams grew louder and louder, Sonny and Cher began to chirp, and then to toot, and finally to screech along with him. *Hate you! Liar! Hate you! Boy!*

"I HATE YOU!"

I sat down on the floor next to him. Then, when he kicked me again, I wrestled with him, covering his body with my own. I could feel the back of his ribs pushing into mine while he squirmed and struggled against me, his arms flailing around, slapping and scratching me. As he bucked against me, I tried to explain. "She's dead, Danny," I said as he continued wriggling and writhing, butting me with his head and kicking me with his knees as I struggled to smoosh him into being still.

"I saw her myself. And me and Gabriel, we buried her." He wriggled free for a second and kicked me again, but I flipped him over, pulling his arms behind him and pinning him there, on the floor, like a butterfly. Then I explained, as best I could, why we'd done what we'd done. "We had to. Because if they find out that you and me are alone, they'll come and take us away, put us in an institution where they beat you every day and don't give you enough to eat, and we wouldn't be allowed to see each other."

"You liar!" he repeated, trying once again to kick me from behind, but I tightened my grip on his arms, pulling them back like I was going to tie his hands behind him.

Just then Gabriel let himself in at the back door, walked through the kitchen, and, seeing us rolling around on the floor, said, "It's true, my little man."

"You lie!"

"We wouldn't do you like that," Gabriel said, his big booming voice thundering over me and Danny, who was still squirming and trying to bite me, until I lost it and was crying and screaming at once.

"Mamma! Mamma! My mamma!"

That's when Danny's body went slack, and I could tell that he finally believed me.

"It's a true fact," Gabriel said from where he still stood, just inside the kitchen.

"It can't be."

"I'm sorry," Gabriel said.

"Then I want to see," he said. "Show me where you put her. You show me."

"Can't," I told him. "I can't take you there."

"Why not?"

I started to tell him that it would be dangerous if he knew, but then I had a terrible thought: That dog last night, that little mangy stray with the pointy ears? He wasn't alone. No sir. There were all kind of stray dogs in our neighborhood, and one thing stray dogs were always looking for was something to eat. I didn't even want to think of it, but every time I closed my eyes, I saw it—black dogs and brown dogs, short dogs and tall dogs, all of them with their sharp, pointy teeth sniffing around that house.

"What is it?" Danny said.

"Nothing," I said, rolling off him.

"What we going to do now?"

"I don't know," I said. "I'll think of something. In the meantime, we've just got to act normal. Like tomorrow? We're going to go to school like normal, take the bus like normal, do everything normal. And then we'll see. We'll come up with something."

"We'll think of something *together*," Gabriel added as he sat down on the sectional. He reached into his pockets and brought out three sandwiches wrapped in plastic wrap. "Here," he said. "I got one chicken salad, and the others are ham and cheese."

I still didn't have any appetite, but Danny was ravenous, devouring his entire sandwich and half of mine as Gabriel sat there telling us how, together, we were sure to think of some plan or another to keep us going. "Trust me," he said. "I have experience with this. Experiential expertise. From life experience."

"But James!" Danny said, burrowing his face into my chest. "How we going to do anything without Mamma? Who's going to take care of us? Who's going to take care of *me*?"

"I will," Gabriel said.

"Me too," I said. "I promise."

But I woke up screaming that night and had to go to the bathroom and splash water on my face to wake all the way up out of my nightmare. In the morning, I saw that Danny had curled himself into a little ball and was sucking his thumb like a baby.

That week just crawled by, as sticky and slow as melting butter. Every morning, I'd wake up and think, just for a second, that Mamma was down the hall making breakfast and everything was normal, but then I'd hear Danny breathing beside me and remember. Somehow, though, we kept on. By the end of the week, we'd come up with a plan.

The plan wasn't actually much of a plan, but it was better than nothing. We were going to continue acting normal. If any of Mamma's friends came over with something for Mamma or wanted to talk to her, we'd say that she was out. But truthfully, Mamma had been feeling so poorly for such a long time that most her friends had stopped coming by anyway. As for her job, every time Supercuts called asking for Mamma, I simply pretended that they had the wrong number. After a while, the calls stopped. There was still plenty to eat in the kitchen, and when that ran out we'd go to the store. There was over eighty dollars left in Mamma's coffee can, and some more money in her wallet too. So I figured that if both Danny and me got an extra roll at lunch at school and maybe swiped an extra apple or banana, too, we could make that money stretch out a long time. And by then we'd have figured something else out.

It was Gabriel who, right away, saw the hole in our plans. "Eighty bucks, let's see . . . that will last you two weeks if you're lucky. Works fine if you want to starve to death." He sniffed in the air, looking hungry, and then tapped the side of his

"Just for starters," he said, getting up and going over to the window where the old air-conditioning unit was thumping and bumping away like it always did, "you got to cut the AC here. I know it's hot. But air? Air alone will run you one hundred dollars a month, *easy*." Without asking, he switched it off. Then he started rolling some other facts and figures out, telling us about tax collections and social security payments and all kinds of things that I'd heard of but didn't know about, adding and subtracting and multiplying numbers in his head, then adding something he called "random factoring" and then coming up with even more numbers, which he announced every few seconds, as if he were giving a report on the radio. It was like getting hit on the head—or rather, in the ears—by a cascade of numbers. Even when Danny, clutching my hand, started sniffling, Gabriel just kept calculating and figuring.

Finally, though, Danny began to sob, and Gabriel, looking at him like he'd only just noticed that he was there, stopped talking. Danny was still wearing the same school uniform he'd worn to school the day after Mamma died, because he had only two total and I hadn't done any washing. The fact is, I didn't know how to do laundry, and anyway, with the washing machine not working, Mamma had started taking our clothes to the Supercuts and washing them there. I hadn't bothered putting our dirty clothes in the hamper, either. Danny and I just left our dirty clothes all over the floor. Danny's white school uniform shirt was covered with gravy and chalk dust, and his knees didn't look too fine, either; they were gray and scabby, as if he'd fallen and scraped his knees and then picked at them until they bled. "We gotta call someone," Danny said. "We're going to starve to death."

"Now, now, little scooter," Gabriel continued, sitting down. Leaning forward with his elbows resting on his knees, he looked like a cross between a talk show host and an elephant. He wore baggy black pants, a yellow T-shirt at least two sizes too small, and the kind of running shoes you get at Walmart because you're too poor to buy Nikes or New Balance. Even so, his posture was confident. "Listen up. You go tell and next thing you know, the police will be here, wham, bam, slam. Next thing, you'll be living in foster care, and you do not want that. No indeed. Trust me. Foster care? More like torture care. They lock you up, and you'll never see your brother again. And you're lucky if they beat you only once a day." He shook his head as if trying to shake off a bad dream.

"Now here's how I see it," he said, recovering. "First, we've got to find a way into your mother's bank account. Second, we've got to get ahold of her bankbook and other things like that—driver's license, credit cards. You know, *documents.* Social security. Birth certificates. Voter registration."

"What's voter registration?" Danny asked.

"You let me worry about that," Gabriel said. Then, turning to me, he asked, "You figure your mamma has money in the bank?"

I said I didn't know for sure, but I did know that she got one hundred dollars in crisp twenty dollar bills out of the

Chase Bank on the corner of Main and Evangeline every Monday morning. "Plus," I said, "She and Daddy were saving up. For our college funds."

"That's a good sign," Gabriel said.

"Yeah," Danny said. "Lila was supposed to go to college, too, but she ran away and got married."

"And you still don't know where she's at?"

"No idea."

Gabriel let out a long, low whistle. "Are you going to go to college, James?"

Was I? That had been the plan, of course. For as far back as I could remember, Mamma talked about how I was going to go to LSU. But now? I wasn't even sure about high school. Even so, I couldn't help but see myself grown-up and walking under those big old spreading oak trees up on that big green campus. I pictured myself walking with a girl, only for some reason she's not a girlfriend, just a friend, and the two of us talking about the kinds of things college students talk about— mainly books, but other things, too, like how many stars are in the sky and how cells divide. Then I thought about Lila, how she was supposed to have gone to college by now, become a nurse or a lawyer, but instead had run off with Zip.

Even before I felt my face getting hot, Gabriel started in on me. "College *man*, college *man*," he said in a singsong. I wanted him to stop. How could he think he was funny when Danny and I were in such a fix? But like usual, he didn't seem to notice that Danny and I were in no mood for stupid. "College man, gon' go get you your degree, do your A-B-C.

College *man*, study all night long, get it right not wrong. College *MAN*, hitting all them books, getting all those looks. *COLLEGE MAN*, smart between the ears, drinking college beers. *COLLEGE MAN—*"

"Shut up!" Danny said.

"Aw, now, little scooter—"

"What's wrong with you?"

Gabriel gave a little shake of his shoulders, and for a moment, I thought he was upset. But all he did was say, "Me, I'm aiming to go to the police academy."

"Who cares?" Danny said.

Gabriel didn't answer. His eyes drifted around the room, finally landing on each of our faces, as if seeing for the first time that Danny and I were just sitting there, four eyes dripping water. "I don't know," he said softly, sinking further and further into himself, like a collapsed balloon.

But a second later he was back on track, talking about how the first thing we needed to find out was how much money was in the bank. After that, he said, we had to find out a way to get to that money, because no bank teller in the world was going to believe me if I said that my mother was too sick to get out of bed and from now on I was getting all the cash money out of the bank, thank you, ma'am. We thought about it and thought about it until finally Gabriel realized that we wouldn't need to be going into the bank at all because I could get cold, hard cash directly from the cash machine. The only problem with that plan was that you needed a password to operate the cash machine; you couldn't just go and put your card in and tell the screen "Give me a hundred dollar, please" and expect the screen to understand you. So that plan was out, too, because no matter how hard I searched—going through Mamma's wallet, including all the secret compartments where she kept little slips of paper, and going through the kitchen drawers, and the little book where she wrote things to herself so she wouldn't forget them—I couldn't come up with any password. That didn't stop Gabriel from taking Mamma's card and trying to get cash with it himself, guessing that maybe she'd used one of our names for the code, or maybe our house number, or our telephone number, or even her birthday. (I told him what it was.) He tried all our birthdays, too, including Grandma's and Lila's, but none of them worked. Then he tried different variations of our social security numbers, which we got off some other papers that Mamma kept in the desk. Then he tried everything else he could think of. Because, like I said, in some respects, Gabriel's brain was made of rubber cement, but when it came to numbers? He must have had a miniature calculator in there. For all that, he couldn't crack the code.

Even with all the windows open, that night it was so hot that I couldn't fall asleep at all. Then when I did, I dreamed again about dogs. Danny shook me awake, saying, "You got one of your nightmares again . . ."

7

THE MASTER PLAN

Like I said, I was in tenth grade that year. I know that everyone does it and that it isn't a big deal, but for me, moving up into the *middle* of high school was kind of like being in a country where I didn't know the natives and, even though I'd been speaking it all my life, I wasn't fluent in the language. Plus the girls? Suddenly all the girls I'd known since kindergarten were a whole new and another class of girls, some of them so pretty that you'd lose your mind just thinking about them. At Prescott Middle, I'd been hovering pretty close to falling into the Valley of the Mutants along with other kids who, like me, hung out in the library and weren't real athletic or big or strong. Still and all, Prescott Middle was one thing—but now here I was in tenth grade, when I was supposed to have grown, supposed to have hit my growth spurt and shot up and grown a pair of shoulders and a muscle or two. Instead, I still looked like a little kid, with a scrawny body, glasses, acne, clothes that didn't fit right, private parts with a mind of their own, no parents, and a kid brother who was always hungry. To top it all off, there were six hundred kids in each grade, so many kids that the building wasn't big enough for all of us and they had to pack us into travel trailers like worms.

Another thing about moving up to tenth was now that I was in the main building, I ran into Gabriel all the time. He'd see me coming, and the next thing he's yelling out, "HEY, JAMES! MY MAN JAMES! DUDE! WHAT'S UP, JAMES MY BRO?" It could be downright embarrassing when he put his huge meat-paws around me, practically dragging me down the hall with my head in a headlock under his armpit, and all the other kids laughing and snickering. Because unlike when he'd pounce on me in the ninth grade annex, where he'd be bigger than everyone else, which gave him this weird kind of uncool cool, there were lots of big kids now. There were boys so big and tall and muscular they almost look grown, and girls with full figures, wearing tight dresses and jewelry and makeup. Couples went around all wrapped around each other, making out and talking all kinds of goo-goo. Kids bragging about all the sex they had. Gabriel, however, was merely big: big and awkward and flabby, with arms that looked like giant pink sausages and a face like a Moon Pie.

"Why are you hanging out with that weirdo?" people would want to know.

"I heard he got dropped when he was a baby."

"I heard he's just plain old stupid."

"I heard he used to go to special school."

"Yeah, well," I'd say. "He's just different, that's all." But mainly I didn't say anything. I'd just walk away, and when I saw Gabriel coming toward me, I'd head toward the bathroom or duck against the lockers like I had some serious business to attend to.

And if Mrs. Jessup, who was the principal, was walking down the hall when Gabriel was in one of his moods? Then we'd both catch it. Because the thing with Mrs. Jessup, she wasn't just strict—she was mean. She'd give you a detention just for chewing gum. She'd give you a detention just for having your shirt untucked. And if the top of your butt was coming out of your trousers? She'd suspend you on the spot. Everything about her was mean, from her tight little mouth, to her mean little eyes, to her oversized tortoise-shell glasses. Even her hair was mean: gray and pulled back, like a gray swimming cap, tight on her head. But Gabriel didn't seem to know it. When other kids talked about mean old Mrs. Jessup, he'd just grin and nod, or worse, say something stupid, like "Really?" or "Y'all just don't know her." Gabriel was the only kid in school who didn't straighten up when she came coming. Instead of making himself scarce or pretending to look into his locker, he'd do something downright insane, like go up to her to high-five her or start singing exactly the kind of song that any fool could tell you Mrs. Jessup wouldn't like— some rap or country song he'd heard on the radio. He was in trouble *all the time* with her, but still, all he'd say was "She's not so bad." What I'm saying is, he could be a downright liability.

But I felt bad, too, because Gabriel was . . . well, Gabriel was *Gabriel*, my best friend, and the only person, other than Danny and me, who *knew*. Without Gabriel, things would be even worse than they already were, and things were pretty bad. For one thing, there was the laundry problem. Even though I'd started washing our uniforms in the bathtub, adding soap and stomping on our clothes and then hanging them out to dry, they didn't look clean, not really, and they smelled funny too. Smelled like mold. And it was still so hot that sleeping was hard. Then, in mid-October, we ran out of food.

One day I came back from school to find Danny sitting in the hot living room, staring at the television set and eating a stick of butter.

"What are you doing?" I said.

"I'm hungry," he said. "I'm hungry, and there isn't anything else to eat in this place."

"You're supposed to bring food home from school. That was the plan. Remember?"

"Yeah, well *you* try bringing macaroni and cheese home from school, douchebag."

"What about bread? Didn't they serve rolls? And apples? They always serve rolls and apples. What about *them*?"

"Yeah. Huh. Whatever, James."

"What do you mean? At least you could have put that butter on a *roll*, idiot."

Danny just looked up at me, his lips all greasy from the butter, and his fingernails ragged and shiny with butter, like he'd just gone and gotten his nails done. His eyes looked like two giant pools of burnt butter, his skin looked like browned butter, and his white uniform shirt, which hadn't really been washed since Mamma had died, was speckled and spotted with butter-colored stains. That's when I noticed that he had a cut over his right eye.

"What happened?" I said.

He shrugged. "Like you care."

I went over to the couch and looked at him. His eye was swollen, and there were little specks of blood on his cheek. "What happened?" I asked again.

"Kid hit me," he said.

"Why?" Danny shrugged.

"Happens all the time in that nigger-filled school."

I flinched. It was one thing, hearing that word on the street or in school. But Mamma, she taught us never to say that word, not ever, not even if someone was going to pay us to say it, saying that she'd been raised to respect everyone— white and black, it didn't matter—and that the schools were for everyone, that they'd been integrated back when she was little, and that there was enough hatred in this world without any one of us adding to it.

"What kid? You have to report him." I looked at Danny again, taking in the way his wing bones jutted out of his back and how his thick mud-colored curls shone like they had butter on them too. "You shouldn't use that word, either. That's just racist talk. Trash talk. That's all about hate."

"*That's all about hate*," he mimicked in a singsong, before changing back into his normal voice. "What gives you the right to tell me what to do? Who made you my boss? How do I even know that you're my brother? Huh?"

"Well," I said. "I am. I'm your brother."

"Well, let me tell you something then, *brother*. I'm hungry. I'm hungry all the time. Kids see me taking apples and—" and here he stopped himself, I don't know why exactly. "They see me taking things, they tell me I smell, that my armpits stink, that I smell like piss, and next thing I know, I'm getting beat on."

Danny was so angry he was shaking, but Cher and Sonny must have thought something funny was going on, because they started to shriek: *College man! I love you! College man!*

"You got to report those kids," I said. "Or at least, you got to report the kid who hit you."

"Yeah, and then he goes and tells the world about our little dining plan. Plus, next time, he'll *really* beat the crap out of me."

"Danny," I said. "You best start telling me what's going on."

"Go away, James," he said. "You're not my mother." And with that, he went back to eating his butter and staring at the TV.

I hadn't told anyone about how hungry we were—not even Gabriel. I don't know why I didn't tell anyone, but part of the reason is that I worried that if people knew we were hungry, then they'd figure out pretty quick what was going on. I was hungry too, so hungry that sometimes all I could do was think of food, and weekends were even harder. I knew I could probably take some of Mamma's stuff down to the pawn shop and get cash, but the thought of pawning her jewelry or her birds . . . well, I just couldn't do it, is all. As for watching TV? It was torture—all those advertisements for Pizza Hut and McDonald's: those big, juicy burgers.

That night was the first time I went out looking for food. It wasn't completely dark out yet, but in-between, kind of pinkish-grayish, with enough light to see but not enough that people would notice a scrawny kid picking through the garbage. First I headed to the Burger King, waiting around outside until I saw some kids throwing their french fries into the trash. When no one was looking, I went over there and got them out. Waited around a little more, and this man throws out half a hamburger. Waited a little more, and I got me some hot apple pie, some chicken, and a cup filled nearly to the top with Coke. Waited a bit more, and someone comes out of the back of the Burger King and throws all kinds of stuff into a dumpster. When no one was looking, I climbed all the way up in there and found all kinds of good things to eat: bags of buns that had only a little mold on them, uncooked frozen potatoes, mushed-up apple pie, nothing wrong with it at all. I brought it all home, and Danny and I ate until we were stuffed. That was my very first time, dumpster diving.

Finally, Gabriel announced that he had come up with something he called the "master plan." He was so excited about the plan that you would have thought he'd won the lottery. "I figured out all the whys and wherefores. I got it all in my head. I came up with a master plan so masterful that nothing can go wrong once we get it in place." All we needed, he said, was to find a woman who looked even a little like Mamma. "And I know just the place to find one." This time, he said, it would be foolproof.

He just couldn't *stop* talking about it.

"We're going to get you all fixed up, organized and established. You'll see, bro," he said, smack in the middle of the hallway between classes. "We gonna get this system up and *running*, and then it's all going to go down so smoothly. You and little scooter will be able to live in y'alls' house and do what you got to do and no one's gonna bother you, not now, not ever."

"Oh yeah?" I whispered, hoping that no one had overheard him.

"We just got to find the exact right woman."

"You think?"

"Just you wait, dog. Once I find her—and I'm *gonna* find her—we'll get the master plan launched *good*, and then things are going to improve, most definitely." Running his tongue along his lips, like maybe he was licking salt off them, he said it again, only louder, "MOST DEFINITELY."

I sure hoped so. We were desperate.

Even though, with my food foraging, we weren't going hungry anymore, Danny was changing, and any fool could see it. Before Mamma died, he was this cute little kid, all goofy and funny, sleeping with Bow-Wow and watching cartoons on TV every chance he got. He loved Bart Simpson, wanted to be just like him. He'd sit there on the sectional, laughing his head off. But now? He was like a scared, hungry mongrel, sniffing around, ready to rip your throat out if he had to. It was like he was growing backward. With every passing day, he was a day younger, a day dirtier, a day whinier, a day more cry-babyish. He was in seventh grade and was supposed to be reading and writing good, reading real books with long paragraphs and chapters, and doing algebra, Louisiana history, science—all kinds of things. But instead, every day he'd come home with all his homework marked up with angry red marks and bad grades. He couldn't do basic arithmetic, division and multiplication, and when it came to writing? All of a sudden, he couldn't spell at all, not even easy words like *water* and *color* and *speaking* that I was sure he knew how to spell.

I'd look through his schoolwork, shaking my head. "Danny," I'd say, "what's going on with you? You're smart, but you're acting dumb. I know things are bad now, and it's hard to concentrate, but you've still got to *concentrate*. What's with you?" And Danny would just set his mouth in a straight line, cross his arms over his chest, and say something like "What makes you think you can be all up in my business, asshole?"

And even with my picking through the garbage like I was doing—I'm not saying I was proud of myself, but I got to be pretty good at hitting the dumpsters up at just the right time, coming home with all kinds of half-eaten food, some of it still warm—Danny still complained about being hungry. Complained all the time. Complained about his clothes being dirty, complained about being hot, complained about being cold.

It didn't help that in school we were reading *Lord of the Flies,* which is the worst book ever. It's all about this group of boys who get stuck together on a deserted island and end up killing pigs and torturing each other and finally going on a killing spree. And all because they were *hungry,* see? Plus, I'd already read it.

It wasn't that I didn't like to read, either—I loved to read. But now, I was too hungry and hot and worried to do much of anything other than do my homework and watch TV, and half of the time I couldn't even do that. My mind wouldn't focus; the words danced on the page before me. My grades were going downhill. Sometimes I even had trouble understanding what was on the TV.

Finally the day came when Gabriel sprung into action. Danny and I were both dreaming, sleeping like we always did in that little back room, rolled up in the sheets, when we heard the sound of tapping on the bedroom window—*tap tap tappety tap.* Danny was curled up beside me, hugging Bow-Wow and sucking on his thumb. All our dirty clothes were spread out all over the place and lying around in heaps. Even though it was morning, I was already exhausted, and when I heard that *tappety tap tap,* I sat straight up, my mind whirling with all the things I had to do. I had to remember to feed the birds and give them fresh water, only their cage was getting nastier and nastier, filled with bird droppings and the shells of bird seed and dirty feathers and bits of dust. I knew I had to take those birds out of their cage and somehow make sure they didn't fly away so I could clean their cage out. I had to make sure there was something for us to eat. I had to find a way to clean some of our clothes. I had to make sure that Danny brushed his teeth, which lately he'd been forgetting to do, and that he took a shower and wore socks and did his homework and, most of all, that he understood that, except for Gabriel, we couldn't tell anyone about what had happened. I had to do my own homework, too, and find a way to get me some new paper and pens, because even though it wasn't yet November, I was running out.

There was one thing that I was ignoring *on purpose,* though, and that one thing was Mamma's room. It was just how we'd left it after Danny had gone in there tearing things up looking for her. Her handbags and shoes, her scarves and dresses and belts, and all her lady-kind-of-things were scattered in heaps all over the floor and on the bed. But neither one of us had gone in there since that afternoon at the end of September. Just thinking about my mother's things thrown all over the floor like that made me sad all over again. And then

I'd start thinking about that little stray dog with the sharp teeth and pointy nose, and before I knew it I'd feel like there were little pieces of glass in my veins. So I tried not to think about any of it at all. Instead, I tried to stay focused; there was Danny, there was me, there was school, and there was eating— that was all I could keep track of.

Once again, I heard it: *tap tap tap.* What on earth? But it was only Gabriel, staring in through our window. When he gestured to me with the thumbs-up sign, I remembered that it was Saturday, meaning that Danny and I had the whole weekend ahead of us, with no cafeteria lunch and nothing to do but sit around being lonely. I turned back to bed, making a motion with my hand for Gabriel to go away and let us sleep.

"But today's the day!" Gabriel yelped through the screen. "We've got plans!"

"What?"

"Let's move on out!" Gabriel said. "It's now or never."

"What's that big, dumb stupid want?" Danny murmured, half-awake. "Tell him to go away." But Gabriel didn't hear him, and I told Danny to shut up.

Twenty minutes later, the three of us were standing on the sidewalk in front of the Mercy and Grace Center, which was really nothing more than an old grocery store on Main Street that had been fixed up with tables and chairs and a couple of comfortable old sofas. Everyone in the neighborhood knew about the Mercy and Grace Center; you couldn't not know about it. "But for the grace of God," Mamma would say every time we drove by it and saw lines of raggedy people waiting to be fed.

Eventually, when we got old enough to understand, Mamma explained what a soup kitchen was and that the men and women who ate at Mercy and Grace weren't evil or bad, just down on their luck or sick or addicted. Her own sister, she'd say, had been one of them. They slept in shelters and on top of heating grates, in alleyways and under trees and in abandoned houses, or maybe if they had a few dollars they'd pool their money and rent a hotel room for the night. Some of them were crack whores, or worse, which was something I didn't know anything about until Mamma explained the whole mess to me. I'll never forget that, the way she explained the kinds of things people do when they get so low-down and hopeless that they don't even know who they are anymore.

I hated thinking about those women doing bad things for money. But I couldn't stop, either. It didn't help that so many kids were already doing things, and bragging on it too. *Hooked up*, they'd say, or *scored big*. And this one girl? This girl, Kia, in my math class? She was so, so pretty, with smooth long hair, long delicate fingers, and a figure that made me burn at night, and sometimes during the day too, making me feel like I had to go to the bathroom all the time. I sat right behind her, wouldn't you know it, staring at the back of her head, the way her hair fell over her neck and how her gold earrings hooped through her earlobes. She was smart, too, Kia was; knew all the answers. But I was too shy and worried to do anything but sit there and stare at the back of her neck. And even if I had worked up the courage to talk to her? I already knew what would happen: she'd take one long, good look at me and decide that I was too raggedy, too dirty, too scrawny, too pathetic, too weird, and altogether too not right to have anything to do with me at all. And frankly, who was I kidding? Even if Mamma and Daddy were still alive and everything was the way it had been, I'd *still* be a total nerd—so awkward and spastic, with my skinny legs and big glasses. No pretty girl in the world would want to hang with me.

"Check it out," Gabriel said, inclining his head in the direction of the line that had already formed in front of the Mercy and Grace Center. The three of us were crouched behind a scraggly little tree that looked like it wanted to cry. "You see her?"

"See who?" As best as I could make out, there were just two women in the group, and neither one of them looked the first thing like Mamma. One was fat-fat, the kind of fat that looks like you're wearing a mattress under your skin, and the other one had hair cut short like a boy's and big red earrings.

"That one there," Gabriel said, pointing. "The one in the black T-shirt and jeans. What do you think?"

"I think I'm hungry," Danny said. "And I want to go home. This is stupid. And you're a dumb ass, numb nuts."

"Don't talk like that," Gabriel said. "Where'd you learn to talk like that?"

"Why? You some kind of faggot?"

Gabriel ignored him.

"See her?" he said.

I looked again, but I didn't see who Gabriel was talking about. "She's a little skinnier than your mother was, I'll give you that as a natural observation observed through the lenses of my vision apertures—in other words, my eyes. And maybe she's a little, I don't know . . . kind of trashy looking. But I've been seeing her and seeing her. Just about every day she's here, first thing. And I don't know. There's just something about her that reminds me of your mamma."

"What you mean you've been seeing her every day? You've been coming down here every day?"

Gabriel shrugged, giving me one of those *who, me?* expressions, like he always did when he was reaching for one of his fancy words but couldn't quite grasp onto it.

"Someone's got to be on the lookout for you," he finally said. "Someone's got to make an executive decision. Seriously. She's the one. Check her out."

I looked one more time, and this time I spotted her. She was fourth or fifth in line, all huddled over, hugging herself as if she was cold, which was unlikely given that it was still only October and the morning air was sticky and warm. South Louisiana is like that. Yet she was breathing on her knuckles and stamping her feet. She wore a short jacket made of a shimmering hot pink material, the tightest pair of jeans I'd ever seen, and red high-heeled shoes, and looked too young to pass as our mother, except she also looked too old. Her fingernails were painted gold.

"Observe her fully, please," Gabriel said. "See?"

I looked again, but all I saw was a fidgety too-young, too-old woman in the kind of fashion jeans that Mamma used to yell at Lila for wearing. And I just knew that, whoever she was and whatever her story might be, she wasn't for us. No sir and no ma'am, not in a million years did a woman who ate at Mercy and Grace and dress like that belong in our lives. "No way," I said. "Let's get out of here."

But Gabriel would have none of it. Poking me in the ribs with one of his fat fingers, he said, "Check out her eyes." That's when, looking at her sideways, I saw it. There *was* something Mamma-like about her, not so much in the way she held herself or how she was built, but around the eyes and jaw and mouth. Sure enough, she looked like she could have been Mamma's sister—or even, if you looked at her just right, Mamma herself, or at least how Mamma looked just before she died.

"We got us a master plan, sure enough," Gabriel said, poking me in the ribs again, but this time with force. "Go on, James. Engage her in conversation."

"*What?*"

"Talk to her, man."

"You talk to her," I said. "I'm not going up to some stranger. I don't even know what we're doing here. So what she looks a little like Mamma? How's some broken-down homeless dipso gonna help me and Danny?"

"James, James, James," Gabriel said, nodding his head real slowly in that annoying way he had. "Have I ever let you down?"

I didn't answer.

8

HOW WE GOT LUCETTA

Gabriel wasn't exactly what you'd call a sharp dresser. That morning, the morning we got up early to go to the Mercy and Grace Center, he looked even goofier than usual: black baggy trousers that swished when he walked, a Minnie Mouse T-shirt that hugged his big belly and massive arms, and black flip-flops that made slapping noises against the sidewalk. As for Danny and me, we were practically still wearing our sleeping clothes. The last thing in the world I wanted was to engage in some kind of conversation with a stranger who looked like Mamma, not dressed the way I was, not *ever*.

But Gabriel pulled both Danny and me into a headlock, one of us under each of his arms, and dragged the two of us right on over toward the entrance to Mercy and Grace.

"Lookee here," one of them beat-up old boozers said.

"Boys, your folks are going to be looking for y'all. Better go on home," another remarked.

But the rest of them just gazed in our direction without seeing us, their eyes big and staring and vacant and half-dead and dull in their centers, smelling like a combination of piss and beer and cigarette smoke. As for the lady who looked a little bit like Mamma, she didn't seem to notice us at all, not even when we were standing no more than two feet away, with Gabriel grinning like he was competing in a grinning contest.

Finally, Gabriel cleared his throat. "Madame," he said.

She didn't move a muscle. Even her eyes didn't move. Even her nostrils.

"Madame!"

It was obvious that she was either too sick or too stoned or too hungover or too all-of-the-above to so much as notice that Gabriel was practically yelling into her face, but Gabriel's enthusiasm wasn't diminished. "Excuse me, ma'am? I'm Gabriel Jones Keyes, and this here is Danny Moore and James Moore."

When she still didn't answer or even look his way, Gabriel shoved the two of us forward with such force that I stumbled, literally falling on her pointy high-heeled shoes.

"Damn!" she said.

"As I was saying, ma'am, these two gentlemen are Danny Moore and his brother, James."

"And I da queen of Egypt," the lady finally said, looking down her face at me like I was dog poop on the bottom of her shoe. "Go on home, boys. Y'all have no business fooling around here." She turned away again, bending double to cough into her hands.

Just then the doors opened, and slowly the little crowd began to move inside. I still didn't know what we were doing there, or how this lady—with her wild-looking eyes and glittery nail polish—could help us. But Gabriel followed right behind, once again pulling Danny and me along with him.

"If we could just talk to you for a minute, ma'am," he said, trailing along while she coughed and blew her nose into a napkin. "If perhaps we might have a conversation."

Finally, she took a good long look at us—me and Danny shoved up under Gabriel's meaty arms, and Gabriel himself, with his shiny skin and goofy clothes and stupid grin.

"Go away."

But Gabriel didn't embarrass easily, and ten minutes later, as the lady sat eating a blueberry muffin, he was right across from her, telling her about his master plan. There was an official-looking man sitting at a little table at the front door, keeping track of things, who kept giving us the eyeball like he knew we were up to something. But the people going around serving coffee and breakfast pastries and little tinfoil cups of fruit didn't seem to notice us at all. In the meantime, Gabriel just kept talking and talking, throwing around all manner of long words and sounding, at least to me, more and more like an outer space mutant. "To have someone such as yourself involved in an official capacity regarding the delicate domestic situation..."

With all that food everywhere, my stomach started to gurgle something awful. Even though I'd managed to keep

Danny and me from starving, other than the food we got at school we hadn't eaten anything new or fresh in weeks. It was all I could do not to sit on down with those junkies and drunks and help myself to some muffins and coffee cake. Looking over, I could tell that Danny was thinking the same thing. The next second, I saw him swipe up a half-eaten donut off the table and put it in his pocket. I wanted to grab something too. But I was too busy listening to what Gabriel was saying, afraid that, if I didn't pay close attention, he'd open his big mouth and tell the entire room our secret.

"You see," Gabriel explained, finally switching to something more like regular English, "these two individuals here, they're brothers, they're family, and they don't want to be busted up. It's not their fault that all the adults in the family up and died on them. And truthfully, James and Danny can pretty much get on by themselves, you know, independent. But when it comes to money? That's where we've got our problem. Because the fact of the matter is that unless these two boys can get the money in their mother's bank account, well, that's the problem, isn't it? Plenty of money, but no way to get *into* it. *Comprende*?"

"Damn."

"Additionally, we need the *authorities* out of this. Fortunately, I've got it all worked out in my head." Gabriel tapped his temple. "Seeing that these young men have all their mother's clothes and pocketbooks and her wallet and her credit cards and her driver's license, all we need now is a lady who looks enough like their mother—may she rest in peace—to go on down to the bank, maybe once a week or so, just often enough so that these boys have enough to eat and things that they need."

"You've been watching too many movies, boy."

"After that," Gabriel said with a satisfied grin, "we can take care of everything. It's just the cash money we need, but have no way of getting unless someone helps us out." (I couldn't help noticing that Gabriel had gone from talking about Danny and me to talking about "us.") "That's where you come in, see?"

I was sweating into my clothes now, the sweat pooling between my shoulders and down the middle of my back. Danny glanced around and swiped more food, this time a strawberry danish with only one bite taken out of it. I held my breath, ready to go running on out of there if Gabriel so much as mentioned where we'd put Mamma, but Gabriel left that part out.

As he talked on and on, the lady slowly drank her coffee, nibbled on her muffin, and wiped the crumbs from her chin. When she was done, she took a half-smoked cigarette out of a pack, tapped it into her hand, and lit it. Finally, she said, "What do I get out of it?"

"You? You get to live with James and Danny."

"What?" she said. "Who?"

"*What*?" I said.

"That's what I've been trying to explain," Gabriel said, waving me back with a flap of his hand. At the same time, he hunched forward to whisper, "These two fine individual young men standing here. James and his little brother—his tag's little scooter, but his real name's Danny. They got them a big old house with nothing but room, a TV, air-conditioning, everything you could want. And all you've got to do is make sure that no one starves."

"I'm hungry," Danny said.

"It couldn't be a more spacious and lovely home," Gabriel said. "And there's plenty of money in the bank, cash money just lying there. But seeing as my associates are still underage and minor, they need an adult on the premises just to get the cash. After that, we're good to go. And as for you, you don't have to do nothing but make yourself at home-sweet-home."

"What?" I said again, but it was too late.

Squinting through her cigarette smoke, the lady got up, shook my hand, and said, "Pleased to meet you, boys. My name's Lucetta." She took another drag of her cigarette. "Just one thing you got to know. If I'm going to be taking care of little boys, them boys better be minding their manners."

9

DOGS IN THE NIGHT

I was so angry at Gabriel, I wanted to bust his big, fat face in. I wanted to cover him with bruises, make his lips bleed. How did he know that this Lucetta person wasn't going to get all of Mamma's money out of the bank and walk on away with it? How did he know she wasn't planning on inviting all her low-life friends to come live with us? Or what if she wanted to turn our house into the neighborhood drug den? Or invite a man to move in with her? Or steal the TV set and all of Mamma's jewelry and Danny's empty piggy bank while she was at it? Then what?

And what about *me*? How was I supposed to be able to so much as focus on my homework or on getting dressed for school with *her* in the house? What if she took to walking around in her underwear or in only a towel? Nighttime was bad enough as it was. Between not being able to sleep because of the howling dogs outside, not being able to sleep because I couldn't stop worrying, and waking up in the middle of a dream about naked girls, I could barely keep my eyes open the next day. And now this lady, who could have been just about anything, including the most low-down of low-downs, was moving in with us? Just like that? But as we headed home—six blocks north and then three east—I couldn't say any of that; Lucetta was trailing along with us, looking around with her dull, flat gaze and chatting offhandedly about this and that like she went home with three strange boys every day of the week.

"My real name is Rose Lucetta, but most folks call me Lucetta."

"Is that so?" Gabriel said.

"That's because my mother, her name was Rose. It was confusing, so mainly my people called me Lucetta."

"That a fact."

"Or just plain Lu. Sometimes they call me Lu."

"Yes, ma'am," Gabriel said.

"Or Miss Lu. But that would have been back in the day."

"Miss Lu," Gabriel said, trying it out in his mouth.

"And you—big boy. What did you say your name is?"

"Gabriel," he said. "Gabriel Jones Keyes."

"Aright then, Gabriel Jones Keyes," she said. "May as well get one thing clear right here and now. Because I don't care what kind of big man you think you are, what kind of Fruit of the Looms you wear, or how tall you are, or even how old you say you are—you come near me with those meat hooks of yours, I'll kill you dead and call the cops afterward."

"Yes, ma'am," Gabriel said, blushing cherry under his wheat-colored skin, that big dumb grin still spreading his cheeks wide. The thought crossed my mind that maybe he was mentally deficient after all, because why else would he be grinning and shaking his head while she talked to him like that? But as soon as I had the thought, I pushed it away, because, like I've been saying, Gabriel was half-and-half: part human computer and part Martian. But no matter what, he was the only person we had in the whole world, the only one who *knew.* Plus, the boy was incapable of doing anything really bad. It hurt my heart the way she talked to him, like Gabriel would in a million years want to try something with her. I looked at Danny, who was looking at the sidewalk, and then looked at the back of Gabriel's head and then at the sky and then at the neighborhood graffiti. On the walls of an abandoned gas station, someone had spray-painted a giant pink heart, which was surrounded by all kinds of messages: *people power! Punta Get Out. BEAU BEAU LOVE CYNDI B. Down with racism, terrorism, fight AIDS.* But I could barely make the words out. Tears were backing up in my throat, getting ready to spill out of my eyeballs.

"I'm still hungry," Danny whined by my side.

"What'd you want me to do about it?" I said.

"Something," he said. "Anything. This isn't Africa. People aren't supposed to be starving to death in America."

"You aren't starving. I'm fetching food for you every day."

"You call that food?"

"You aren't starving."

Still and all, by then the only thing either one of us could think about was food. Despite our attempts at eating double the amount at lunch and taking food home with us from school, and the food I managed to scrounge from dumpsters, both of us had lost weight. While I never came home empty-handed, that first big dumpster haul had been a onetime only. As time had gone by, I'd had to settle for less: a couple of pieces of chicken nuggets at the bottom of a bag, some hash browns, or the remains of a wilted salad. Me, I could make do on one big meal a day—shoving in the tater tots and the hot dogs, the green beans floating in green bean juice with little pieces of pink meat tossed in, the meat loaf, and the chicken chunks at school and then topping it off at night with whatever I managed to scrounge from what people threw out at McDonald's and Pizza Hut. But Danny must have been hitting a growth spurt, because it seemed that just about the one thing that boy *did* do was complain about hunger pangs.

"I've got to get some food," he said.

"What about that danish you swiped back there? Why don't you eat that?"

"I did," he said.

"You eat that donut too?"

"It was half-eaten already," he said. "It had only two bites left in it."

We continued on like this, in whispers, several paces behind Lucetta and Gabriel, until at last we got back to the house. It looked the same as always—kind of old, but homey, with green bushes along one side, and, out back, the funny little shed that Mamma used to call "the laundry room." White curtains still hung in the two front windows, and the doormat still said "welcome."

"This your place, huh?" Lucetta said as we opened the front door to let her in. She shrugged and looked around, as if she'd seen better.

This your place, this your place, Cher began to sing.

Lucetta didn't seem to notice, but instead she stood in the front room for a while, nodding her head a little, as if in conversation with herself. Then she went over to the TV and turned it on. She poked at Mamma's sectional, turned the TV off, went into the kitchen and tried the faucets, and then went back into the little room where Danny and I slept. "Uh," she said, poking her head in, then "Jesus." In the bathroom, she sniffed at the air like a dog. She went out back, opened the door to the shed, looked at the washing machine and the laundry hamper, and shrugged. Back inside, she stood in front of the cabinet and gazed at the pictures: Mamma and Daddy on their wedding day, Lila graduating from middle school, Grandma and Granddaddy, me as a baby, Danny on Santa's lap. She looked at Mamma's collection of glass birds—the purple one, the yellow one, the one that looked like it was made of clear marbles. Finally, she went over to the birdcage, where Sonny and Cher were squawking, saying, *tweet tweet tweet, I love you! College man! I miss my baby! Help me, Jesus!*

Like I said, those were some smart birds.

But Lucetta didn't say a word. Her face was so still, so fragile, that she could have been a statue. She finally turned to look at us. "Hot in here."

"The boys like to keep the windows open—fresh air and all that."

She grunted. "What did y'all say happened to your ma? She died?"

"Heart attack," Gabriel offered. "Biggest funeral you ever saw."

"No grandparents? Aunties or uncles? Cousins?"

Again, Gabriel answered. "The boys certainly do have relatives. But they live far away. They live in Asia. The other side of the word, you see? So the city of Crystal Springs—meaning the government, the authorities, the specialists, and whatnot— you know, they sent some social workers in. The social workers decided that just as it's nice and legal and the house is paid off, the boys could stay here. In their own house."

"I don't want to be fooling with no social workers."

"But that's just it," Gabriel continued. "Once that social worker—how did they put it? Once she *signed off* here, she never did come back. She told us that she was closing down the case, that everything was fine. So off she goes. How long ago was that?" He looked at me like he was asking me a real question. "Four months ago, right?"

"Something like that," I mumbled. Meanwhile, Lucetta was looking from Gabriel to me to Danny to Gabriel again.

One side of her mouth was propped up a little, like her lips were shrugging. "What do you have to do with all this?" she asked Gabriel. "You a cousin? Or just one of their crew?"

"Just that I kind of like to help these boys out. Being that I'm eighteen, legal and all," he said, lying. "Those social workers? They said it's like I've kind of got—how do they call it?—power of attorney. That means that I get to make decisions for them, legally. All I have to do is sign on the dotted line, give 'em my official signature. It's comprehensive."

Where Gabriel got all this I couldn't say—and anyway, he was sixteen, not eighteen. And as for power of attorney? I didn't know what that meant, but I felt sure that he'd gone too far and Lucetta would figure things out and hightail it out of there, going straight to her street friends to tell them about us. And then the whole pack of them would be hanging out at our house, having parties, and Danny and I would *really* be in trouble. Instead, she just stood there, her face a blank, one hip thrust out, her hands trembling like she was cold. Finally, she spoke. "Mind if I have me a nap, boys?" she said.

"'Course not," Gabriel answered. And the next thing we knew, Lucetta went into Mamma's room, closing the door behind her.

Danny sat himself down on the sectional to watch Saturday morning cartoons, including the ones he was way too old to watch, like *The Incredible Hulk* and *The Heathcliff and Dingbat Show*. When the cartoon shows were over, he switched to PBS and started watching *Sesame Street* and anything else that was on too. *Bill Nye the Science Guy*. *Louisiana: The State We're In*. *Barney*. All kinds of baby shows. Didn't matter. Because even if we still had the computer? Danny would have sat in front of it all day, too, getting up only to go to the bathroom or complain that he was hungry. He was like a giant baby, only worse, because babies aren't mean, and Danny was getting meaner by the minute.

As the day went on and Lucetta didn't get up, I started to worry that she'd already stolen all of Mamma's things and had crawled out the window with them. Either that, or that she'd gone ahead and died too—dying in Mamma's bed just like Mamma had. Dying from the heat. But when I checked, all I saw through the crack in the door was Lucetta, stretched out on the bed, snoring.

"I'm hungry," Danny said.

"What you want me to do about it?"

"Get some food from where you normally get it. Steal it. I don't care."

But I couldn't leave him—not now, not with Lucetta sleeping in the next room and no telling when she was going to wake up. The best I could do was go through all the kitchen cabinets to see if maybe there was something in there that I'd missed. But all I could find was some roach killer and a bottle of Ajax.

"What's she doing in there?" Danny asked.

"Sleeping."

The afternoon was getting on now, the sun rays slanting

longways through the windows, making leafy patterns on the floor and tickling the walls with a wash of pale light.

That year—the year that Mamma died and I started tenth grade at Springs City High—I was five foot and a half inch tall, with skinny arms and legs and a head so big and round that even I knew it looked like a globe. My nose was wide, with nostrils that, to me, looked like twin caves. I wore glasses. No matter what I put on in the morning, I had "geek" written all over me. I looked like a walking advertisement for geekhood. I wouldn't have minded it so much if other things of a more private nature having to do with my manly parts were happening, but they weren't. Boys in school, not just big boys like Gabriel, who looked like he was twenty even though he was only in eleventh, but kids my own age had hair springing off their cheeks and broad shoulders and muscles like all they did all day long was work out at the gym. Talking about sex and bragging that girls were doing all kinds of things with them. I didn't like hearing that kind of talk, but at the same time I couldn't get enough of it. And sometimes at night, when I was falling asleep, I'd dream that Danny wasn't Danny at all, but some girl, some girl with beautiful eyes and long hair. Or maybe I'd dream that he was Kia, the girl who sat in front of me in math. I'd wake up with Danny hitting me, saying, "James! What you doing to me? You some kind of pervert!" And now we had a strange lady sleeping in the next room, in Mamma's bed? How was I supposed to deal with *that*?

She didn't get up at dinner time, either. She didn't get up later, when it began to get dark and all the dogs in the neighborhood started sniffing around and barking toward the sky, barking like they had friends up on the moon. Gabriel came by as it was getting dark and then again later, bringing a can of Coke and a box of Little Debbies. So Danny and I ate dessert for dinner while Sonny and Cher went *Peep peep! Help me, Lord! Tweet tweet! College boy!* They got so loud that it was a downright nuisance, and I had to put a towel over their cage so they'd think it was time to stop talking and go to sleep.

We watched TV some more until finally there was nothing to do but for me and Danny to go to sleep too. Like usual, Danny drifted off right away—he was in a stupor from watching TV and eating all that sugar for dinner—but I lay awake, staring at the ceiling, worrying about Lucetta stealing all of Mamma's things, and trying not to cry.

I didn't want Danny to know how afraid I was. But a few hours later, I woke up screaming and covered with sweat. In my nightmare, the dogs were everywhere, clustering around Mamma's head, chewing on her feet, biting into her eyeballs. One of them lifted his leg and let a long yellow stream fall onto her nightgown, spotting it with large blotches that grew and grew until they were puddles of blood. Then Danny and I were slipping in her blood, falling into the hole under the house, and after us were a pack of wild dogs with big yellow teeth.

"James!" It was Danny, shaking me by the shoulders. "Wake up! You having another one of those dreams." I opened my eyes. Danny's face was outlined by light coming in through the window. "I'm thirsty," he said, and I got up and got him a glass of water. On the way back, I peeked into Mamma's room again and saw the outline of Lucetta's body, her back to me, under the blankets. The moon was shining through the window, and Lucetta's breath was going in and out, in and out, real soft, like a baby's.

10

GABRIEL TELLS US
ABOUT MRS. FOSTER

First thing in the morning, who shows up but Gabriel, wearing a Jaguars hoodie—the kind with a pouch—and black basketball shoes. He banged on the door, a jelly donut in each of his big old paws.

"Good morning, looking alive!" he said when I came out of the bedroom, rubbing my eyes because I didn't know if I was asleep or awake, and didn't much want to know, either. Danny was still in bed, curled up on his side like a newborn kitten. "Rise and shine! We got places to go and people to see."

I ignored him. Inside their cage, the birds were twittering. As soon as I took their nighttime towel off, Cher looked right at me, saying, *College boy! College boy!*

"We've got business to attend to, dude," Gabriel said, ignoring my mood as he finished off his donut in two bites.

"No, we don't," I said.

"Sure we do," he said, going right over my words as if I'd never spoken them at all. "Your girl up yet?" He pointed the top of his head toward Mamma's bedroom door.

"Look like she's up?"

"She's not dead, though."

"How can you say that? How can you joke about that?"

He shrugged. "Sorry."

"You planning on eating that second donut all by yourself?"

"What about it?" he said. But then, perhaps seeing my face go dark, he slapped his big paw on my shoulder and said, "I'm just playing with you." Handing me the donut, he pulled a third one out of the pouch on his sweatshirt, humming to himself.

Right then Danny came out, wearing his Fred Flintstone pajamas and holding onto his old, ratty-looking teddy bear dog. "Who's dead?" he said in a high-pitched voice that sounded like something was stuck in his throat. "Is someone dead? Did she die? James, what's he talking about?" But before I had a chance to explain—as best I could, given that I didn't know any more than Danny did—Danny had burst into Mamma's room, without knocking. I heard a yelp, then an "excuse me, ma'am," then another yelp, and then Lucetta came stomping out of the room wearing Mamma's pink silk bathrobe. It was so big on her that it made her look like a little girl playing dress-up.

"Don't. You. Boys. Know. How. To. KNOCK?" she said.

"Ma'am?"

"Damn! You want me living here and putting my neck on the line getting money out of the bank and pretending to be your mother—y'all know I could be locked up good for something like that, because with what I been doing, well, enough said. But with something like what y'all want me to do? With banks and money? That's only a thousand times worse than some of the things I've had to do just to get by. And don't tell me you don't know what I'm talking about, because I can see it in your faces that you do. That donut for me? Give it here."

She went right up to Gabriel, took the donut out of his hand, and began to chew while Danny watched, his mouth open and dripping saliva. "Doing all this plus other things I already done? I could have my ass locked up, sent on down to St. Gabriel, and you never will see Lucetta again, because I'll be locked up for *good*." She snorted. "So if you want me to do your little errands for you and keep my big old mouth shut about what we're all doing here, then I kindly suggest that you knock on the door before y'all come barging on in, catching me out in my nature suit."

"What?" was all Danny could say.

"A lady needs a little privacy," she said. "Understand?"

We all stood around, listening to Sonny saying, *Damn. This is it? Damn.*

As if in agreement, Lucetta snorted loudly. Her eyes rested on each of us in turn before landing on our birds. "Damn, those birds are loud. They always so damn loud?"

"Yes, ma'am." This time it was Gabriel.

Damn loud, Cher agreed.

"As I said, boys, I need my sleep. Especially if my special friend calls on me."

"What special friend?" Danny asked. "What are you talking about?" I could tell that he was about to explode, so I kicked him to shut him up.

Lucetta looked at me and said, "Nah, boy, don't do your brother like that." Then she sighed. Finally, she crossed her arms over her chest and, sighing some more, looked right at Danny, who by now was blushing purple under his dirty face. "Let's see. How can I best explain it? I've got a gentleman friend is all, Earl. He comes around, likes to see me. He's my— he's my boyfriend, I guess you could say. Steady. Understand?" Danny nodded automatically. "Good then. We're all straight. Only damn, I'm hungry. You got any more donuts? Or maybe you got some waffles? You know, the kind that come frozen in a box?"

Danny and I looked at each other.

"All out," Gabriel said.

"What about another donut, then?"

"That one you ate? That was the last."

"Well," Lucetta said, plopping herself down on the sofa. "I need me something to eat in the morning, and Mercy and Grace is not where I want to be."

The three of us just looked at each other, not knowing what to say. Finally, Gabriel sat up tall, pulling on the hood of his hoodie like a woman arranging her hair: "You heard her. James, go on down to the store and get some Twinkies or something."

"What?"

"You like Twinkies?" he asked Lucetta.

"They're all right."

"Go on," Gabriel said.

"And while you're at it," Lucetta said, "bring me a pack of GPC, mentholated. The kind in the green box. Make sure they're mentholated."

Lord have mercy! I miss my baby!

"I can't buy cigarettes," I said. "You need to be eighteen."

"Well, find some way to get 'em, anyway."

"You heard her, James," Gabriel said.

I was so angry, and so scared, I didn't know my own name. I looked at Gabriel, who was grinning that big old dumb grin of his, and then looked at Danny, who was looking at me as if I were a stranger. I heaved a sigh—and then I opened my mouth: I wanted to tell Gabriel that he'd caused enough trouble and to get on up and out of the house. I wanted to tell him never to come back in, either, and while he was at it, he could take Lucetta with him. I wanted to tell Lucetta to take Mamma's silk robe off and stop ordering me around. I wanted to scream. I wanted to cry. Instead I said, "We hardly have any money left."

"Are you saying it true, boy?" Lucetta said.

"Yes, ma'am."

"I see."

"Yes, ma'am."

"And another thing," she said. "If I'm living here, and it looks like I am, I don't want all this ma'am business. Make me feel old. Don't get me wrong. Your mamma, she sure did teach you good, teaching you good manners and respect. But y'all need to be calling me something other than ma'am."

"Like what?" Gabrielle said.

"Y'all call me 'Miss Lu,'" she said and then, agreeing with herself, nodded. "Don't that sound nice?"

We headed out—all four of us, of course, because Gabriel just had to tag along with us, no matter what. Lucetta said she had a few dollars. Then I said that maybe I could find a little money too, even though I knew we were down to less than six dollars, and I'd been holding it back for an emergency. Gabriel said that he had thirteen dollars or thereabouts in change plus a little more if he looked under the furniture. Lucetta said she wanted herself a real breakfast anyway, saying that she was sick and tired of donuts and orange juice and the kind of crap they give you in the shelters and soup kitchens. "I used to have myself some real food," she explained as we headed out the door. "I'm tired of powdered eggs and instant coffee. Yes, indeed, I used to eat *good*. I wasn't always so skinny. Used to have some flesh on me. Used to cook too. You name it— roasted chicken, ham, cookies. I could cook. All the women in my family could." She kept rambling along like that, talking about food until I could feel the saliva pooling under my tongue and hear my stomach grumbling. Then we came to the intersection of South and Main and found ourselves in front of the Piccadilly. Next to the Piccadilly was a thrift store, and next to that a boarded-up beauty parlor, and next to that a liquor store. There was a Pizza Hut, too, but it was separate, sitting by itself on the corner. A week or so earlier, I'd picked up a partly eaten sausage pizza from one of its trash cans. In its parking lot, cars were already baking under the sun.

"Piccadilly, here we come," Gabriel said. "My favorite restaurant."

"Oh yeah?"

"After you, *mademoiselle*."

Danny and me hadn't been to the Piccadilly since the night Mamma died, when I had taken him out and let him stuff his face. Now he looked like he couldn't decide if it was safe to go in there or not. But as we stood outside, gazing in, I could see his eyes wandering over all that wonderful food, like we were on the doorstep to the Garden of Eden.

"Go on, ladies and children first," Gabriel said, pushing Danny through the door with me just behind. But once we were actually in the line, Danny couldn't decide what he wanted: Eggs or grits? Blueberry muffin or banana muffin or chocolate chip? Sausage? Bacon? He just stood there, staring at all that food, his eyes as big as tires. Finally, he chose, and then I chose, and then all four of us sat down in a booth.

"You always eat like that?" Lucetta asked Gabriel as we set-tled into the booth. That's when I noticed that his plate was heaped up with pancakes. "That why you're so big and fat? Or are you just hungry? You know, what with growing pains and all. You still have growing pains, seeing you eighteen? Probably not. You're all lard as it is."

Now, if it had been me, I would have been insulted. But Gabriel patted his belly like he was Santa Claus and started explaining that because he'd always been hungry when he was a little kid, once he started getting enough food, it was like he could *never* get enough.

"I hear you," Lucetta said.

That's all the encouragement he needed. "The way it was for *me*?" he started in, settling back in our booth and talking between mouthfuls of pancakes and syrup. "Truth? I was just this little kid. Didn't know my right from my left. Coming up in New Orleans. Not so different from here, really, but more shooting. That's what I remember, most . . . just about every night, out my window, *bang, bang, bang*. Sometimes I couldn't sleep because between the shooting outside my window and the partying inside, it was like living inside a boom box. Let me see. I guess my mother was living then. Her name was June—Auntie told me that." He knocked on the side of his head, like he was trying to pry loose a memory. "But then, you know. Things got a little rough, I guess you could say, and the social workers come on in and they take me away. Next thing I know, they were telling me that Mamma had gone and joined my father in heaven but aren't I a lucky little boy, because I get to go live in foster care."

"Uh," Lucetta said.

He puffed out his lips. "Yes, indeed."

Lucetta lit up a cigarette, inhaling slowly, leaving pink lipstick stains on the white filter. "I was raised by my grandmother. She tried—I'll give her that—but my grandmother? Lord have mercy, that woman was mean as a snake."

"My foster mother?" Gabriel said. "Her name was Mrs. Donita Chauvier, and she must have had twelve cats. I was supposed to call her *Mrs. Chauvier* and take care of the cats and say 'please' and 'thank you' and not make any messes. I was just a little kid too. When I forgot, like this one time I forgot to clean out the kitty box, you know, where all those cats went to the bathroom? Well, Mrs. Chauvier didn't like that. So she put me in the closet."

"What you mean, she put you in the closet?" Lucetta was rolling her eyes back in her head as she inhaled and exhaled deeply, letting the gray cigarette smoke pour out of her nose like dragon's breath.

"She put me in the closet, like I just said," Gabriel said, recrossing his big, meaty arms over his chest. "She stuck me in the closet with the broom and the mop and the buckets and all kinds of stuff, and she told me that if I had to go—you know, to *relieve myself*—to use the bucket, and if I missed I'd just have to stay in the closet until I learned my manners."

"Woman should have been locked up herself," Lucetta mumbled.

"First time she locked me in like that, I just cried and cried. I cried until I couldn't cry no more and pounded on the door until my hands started bleeding. *Let me out! Let me out!* It was dark in there, and hot, and smelled bad. Smelled like dead things. And there were cockroaches. I could hear them moving around inside the walls, and sometimes I'd feel one of them climbing on me. But the closet? The closet wasn't even the worst of it."

"Lord, Lord," Lucetta said while Danny continued to shovel eggs and bacon and toast into his face, eating so fast it was like watching a garbage truck scoop up garbage.

"I was hungry all the time too," Gabriel said. "And it got worse from there." Next to me, Danny kept gobbling down his breakfast. As for me, I suddenly felt queasy.

"People sure can be evil," Lucetta said.

"She didn't feed me. That's what I remember most. That feeling of being hungry all the time. Then she'd give me moldy bread that she'd cover with sugar, saying that the sugar made it taste just like cake. Sometimes she'd let me eat off her plate once she was done. So I started eating the cat food, only Mrs. Chauvier caught me and locked me up in the closet again. This time it was for longer. I kept crying *Mamma, Mamma! I want my mamma!* But Mrs. Chauvier, when she did let me out, she'd just tell me that my mamma was locked up good and never would be coming out after all she done."

"Why?" Lucetta said. "Because first off, didn't you say your mamma had already gone up to heaven? And anyway, what did your mamma do that was so bad? Check forging? Drug dealing? Rob a bank? Murder?"

"I don't think so," Gabriel said. And then, almost as an afterthought, "Anyway, like you prognosticated a moment ago, she was already completely dead."

"Good God!" Lucetta murmured. "There sure are a *lot* of dead mammas around here."

That's when Danny burst into tears. It wasn't quiet crying either—like the way some ladies do when they watch sad movies—but loud and out of control. *Waagh! Waagh!* You would have thought that someone had chopped his arm off right then and there, that's how much he was carrying on. "I want my mamma! What you do with Mamma, James? How come you won't let me go see her? Where's my mamma! It's *your* fault, James, your fault, and now they won't let me see her, and I'm hungry all the time, and I don't understand multiplication, and I WANT *CLEAN CLOTHES!*"

All around us, people were staring without trying to look like they weren't staring. Some of the older people, men and women both, were shaking their heads and making *tsk-tsk* sounds.

"Hush up," I kept saying. "Not now. Not here." But Danny, he just kept on wailing louder and louder, making me more and more nervous, because what if there were police in the restaurant, or people from social services? What if they came over and started asking questions? "Hush your mouth," I hissed, squeezing Danny's wrist under the table. But his wailing only grew worse, until at last Lucetta leaned over the table and smacked him one.

It was the strangest thing. Even though I'd wanted to do the same thing for the longest time, seeing Lucetta slap him like that made me feel so angry that I began to shake inside. And even though I didn't say anything, I could feel my throat constrict and knew that I wouldn't be able to talk without my voice breaking into trembles.

"What'd you do that for?" Danny said.

"Boy," she said, shaking her head as if she were in pain, "you're just way too loud for Miss Lucetta this early in the morning. Now me and you? If we going to get along? No screaming and hollering at the Piccadilly. You understand?"

"Yes, ma'am," Danny said.

"And no *ma'am* either," she said. "Sure, it's polite. But didn't you hear what I just be saying about not wanting to feel like some old lady?"

"Yes, Miss Lu," he said.

"That more like it," she said, grinning.

It was only later that I realized that Gabriel still hadn't told me how he'd ended up living with his auntie in Crystal Springs.

11

LUCETTA SHOWS US HOW TO DO THE LAUNDRY

Danny was still sniffling when we got back to the house, but he'd calmed down. Plus, with his belly full, it was like all the springs in him had settled, relaxing into a state of let's-see. But I was getting more and more upset. My mother and father? They weren't perfect. I mean, they did a lot of stuff that just downright made me crazy. Like if I talked back, even a little, even if I was joking? Mamma would grab me by the jaw and just *look* at me until I apologized. And if she wasn't satisfied with the way I apologized the first time, she'd just keep holding on to my jaw, squeezing, like I was a bug that she was trying to crush. But one thing she never did was hit. Which was funny, because Crystal Springs? Everyone was hitting their kids, and I mean *all the time*. Kid talk back? *Whap*. Kid throw attitude? *Slap*. Act up in the Walmart or the Albertsons or in church? *Smack*—kid is backhanded into Alabama.

"Miss Lu?" Danny said once we were all sitting around again in the house, doing nothing because it was Sunday and there wasn't anything we *could* do other than listen to Cher and Sonny yammering on like they did.

"What do you want?" she said.

"You need anything, maybe a glass of water, Miss Lu?"

"Well, I'll be damned. You boys sure do have some beautiful manners. But no, darling, I don't need nothing."

Help me, Jesus! College man!

Lucetta pushed back against the sofa cushions. "Your mother must have been some fine lady, teaching you boys so good. Shame, her passing like that. But me and you"—she was looking directly at Danny now, with a smile on her lips—"I'm thinking that we're gonna get on fine. 'Specially now that we know what's what in the morning. Only I got me a question."

"Miss Lu?" This time it was Gabriel.

"Didn't she teach you none about keeping house? I seen flophouses better kept than this place. Golly damn, I done seen junkyards better than this."

"What's a flophouse?" Danny said.

"Where people go when they get so low there ain't no lower," Lucetta said matter-of-factly. "Y'all want me to stay, then you got to clean up some of this mess. Starting with this here birdcage. Because this place? This place so downright disgusting it smells." She waved her hands up and down, to indicate the jumble. Her gold fingernails glittered in the dusky light coming through the windows, and her rings sparkled.

"And if there's one thing Miss Lu can't much tolerate, it's bad smells. Like some of these men I meet at Mercy and Grace? Lord have mercy, some of them smell worse than the Exxon refinery."

She stopped, noticed that Danny was staring at her, and started again. "Speaking of bad smells, when was the last time y'all boys took a bath?"

I could feel myself blushing to the roots of my hair. It was true what she said; both Danny and I were getting kind of rank. But there wasn't much we could do about it, not with the heat being what it was and our not being able to run the air conditioner. Because the heat of a South Louisiana fall isn't like no other heat there is: not like a hot shower, or the warm feeling of being in front of a heater on a cold day, or even the feel of the sun when it gets trapped in a car. By early fall it was like the whole city had simply given up, wilting and crumbling and fading under the sun. The trees had taken on a limp, brownish, droopy look, like all the color had been leached from the leaves. The houses looked tired. Even the tar on the streets didn't shine, but just lay there, colorless, like rubber cement. And even now that it was getting on toward winter, we hadn't caught a break. Days were hot and nights were worse, because at least in the day you could duck inside a store or a McDonald's for a blast of AC. And the mosquitoes? You go outside at night, and by the time you get back *inside* you just better have a gallon or two of Calamine lotion and another couple of gallons of Bactine.

Lucetta got up, scowled, and went over to visit with Cher and Sonny. "When was the last time anyone changed this bird-cage here?" she said.

"We've been feeding them every day," Danny piped up. "Giving them water too."

"Yeah, but you got to change their newspaper. This here cage is nothing but bird droppings." She lit up another ciga-rette. "And me getting into this here mess," she said, almost to herself. Then she looked at Gabriel. "You. You take this here cage outside and clean it out good, hear me? And then put some new newspaper or paper towel on the bottom of it. And don't be *messing* with these birds, neither. These birds are *beautiful* birds, and I don't want your paws all over them hurting them none or letting them fly away, you hear?"

"Yes, ma'am. Only?"

"Only what?"

"How can I make sure they don't fly off?"

"What are you, stupid?" she said. "Take them on out of there, real careful, and put them somewhere where they can't fly off, hear?"

"Like where?"

"Damn boy, you think I know?" Lucetta said, but you could tell she was thinking about it anyway, so I wasn't sur-prised when she told him to put them inside the laundry hamper. "They can't get out," she said, "but they can breathe."

"Mamma loved those birds," Danny said. His eyes were round and solemn and dark and scared. His head was too big on his skinny neck. And his beaky nose, curved like Cher's and Sonny's beaks, quivered.

"I'm going to help you take care of them birds," she said. "But I ain't your maid, got it? If I'd a wanted to be a maid, I could have done signed up for being a maid, like my mean old mawmaw wanted. She said I wasn't fit for nothing else. Said that the best I could do was work at a hotel, cleaning up after the hotel guests. Guess what? I did what she told me to do. When I finished school, I went and got myself a job working at the Holiday Inn, working for minimum wage for a nasty manager who was always trying to grab some. One day I had enough and quit. That life wasn't for me. It was downright boring, for one thing. And from that day to this I've refused to do that kind of work. So let's get this straight—I'm not your maid, I'm not your cook, and I sure enough am not your mamma. But looking like I'll be staying a while, I think we can all agree that if we do things together, we'll get along fine."

"Miss Lucetta?"

"What do you want now?"

"I sure could use some clean underwear."

No one said anything. Even the birds stopped talking. But then Lucetta put her hands on her hips, threw her head back, and started laughing like it was the funniest thing she'd ever heard. It was then that I noticed that she had a scar running faintly from behind her left ear to halfway to the middle of her throat. Her gums were almost purple, and she didn't have much in the way of back teeth. "Dang, boy," she said when she was done laughing. "You're too much. Lord have mercy."

College boy! Dang, boy!

Personally, I didn't see what was so funny. But something about what Danny said, or how he said it, must have gotten to Lucetta. The next thing I know, she was on her feet, ordering everyone around, directing us to pick up all our dirty things—not just the clothes, but the towels and washcloths and whatnot too—and then she started separating things into dark colors and light colors, all the while muttering about how she never had wanted to be anyone's mother and didn't want to start now.

"I been telling you and telling you," she mumbled to herself as we worked, "I'm not doing that. No indeed, I don't right like being treated like that, not by no Earl, not by no one." The more she paced, the more she talked, holding long conversations, only she was the only person doing the talking. She sure as heck wasn't talking to us. Mainly, it seemed, she was talking to Earl. She was angry at him. She was also talking to her grandmother, saying, "Sure enough, Mawmaw, I know you wanted me to be better, but what am I supposed to do?"

Suddenly she looked up and seemed to realize where she was. "What are y'all looking at?" she said.

"Nothing."

"Must have been talking to myself again. Don't mind me none, hear?"

Then, as if she were switching the channels inside her

head, she got up and, looking around, made us take all the sheets off all the beds and empty the trash cans. She told us to sweep out the house and then sweep it out again. When Gabriel brought Cher and Sonny back inside, she made him take them back outside for some fresh air, and then made him grab some rags to wash down the counter. She ordered him to grab the broom and sweep along the window ledges. She told Danny to wash the sink out and told me to take some Ajax and wash the toilet and the bath. She made me open up Mamma's case and wipe down the glass birds with Windex until they sparkled. "Those things are almost as beautiful as real," she said. "Birds everywhere in this house."

Once Lucetta was satisfied, we hauled all our dirty laundry out of the house and started walking towards Main Street. When no one was looking, Lucetta pulled a tiny screwdriver out of her purse and jimmied a parking meter until out poured quarters—dozens of them, all round and shiny. "Don't tell no one, boys," she said. "Just a little trick of the trade." At the laundromat, we put all that dirty laundry in three big washing machines, Lucetta paying with the swiped quarters. She showed us how to measure out the laundry soap and put it in, and what buttons to push. It was easy. "Learn how to do it right, because y'all are going to be doing this job in the future without Miss Lu," she said. By midafternoon, the laundry was clean, the birdcage had new newspaper, Cher and Sonny were blinking their eyes and chirping, and Lucetta was smiling a big, wide smile.

"Well, it's no mansion in a magazine," she said, "but it'll do."

"Nothing like home!" Gabriel piped up.

"Only one thing left to do," Lucetta said. "And that's to turn on the air." And just like that, she'd turned the air-conditioning unit back on, setting it down to cold. "That's better," she said, plopping herself down on the sectional like she'd lived with us all her life.

"But Miss Lu," I said, "we had to turn that off. We can't pay our electric."

"These boys don't need anyone coming after them for it," Gabriel added.

"I thought you said your mamma had plenty of money in the bank, isn't that right?" Lucetta said. "Because no Miss Lu is going to be living here without air-conditioning. No, indeed."

"She's right," Gabriel said as he let himself out the door. "Let the lady have her comforts."

With that, Lucetta smiled again. But she still couldn't sit still. She got up, walked over to the window, and lit a cigarette. She picked up the phone, put it down, and went over to the TV. She turned it on, sat down, and flipped through the channels. As she changed channels, her whole body seemed to be dancing, dancing inside itself, her fingers and toes, her eyelids, her nostrils, even her shoulders were quivering. Suddenly she stood up, grabbed her purse, and headed for the door.

"Y'all be good," she said. "I'll be back when I get back."

Danny and I just looked at each other. Good thing we'd had such a big breakfast because we both knew we weren't getting anything else to eat that day unless I fished us out some leftover half-eaten chicken bones or burgers. We watched TV for a while, and then I told Danny to do his homework. While he was doing that I went over to Gabriel's house to see if maybe I could rustle something up to eat. Gabriel's auntie was at work, and Gabriel gave me a whole package of hot dogs. So it turned out that Danny and I did okay after all, especially seeing as how anyone can cook hot dogs. Around dinner time I made Danny take a bath, and then we sat on the front steps for a while. Finally, I took a bath too.

Even though it was still early, we both got into bed. For once the bed didn't smell like sweat or candy wrappers or Doritos. With the air-conditioning on in the living room, the whole house had cooled down, and for the first time since Mamma died I didn't feel like I was covered in sticky goo. I tried not to think about how we were going to pay for the electric. I tried not to think about anything. But Danny wouldn't let me. "What you think?" Danny said as he snuggled up with his dog who was really a teddy bear. "You think she'll be back?"

"I don't know."

In the distance was the sound of rain coming on and of dogs barking and cars passing by. In the living room, Cher and Sonny were chirping, but then they stopped, and we all fell asleep.

12

LILA SENDS A POSTCARD

The next morning, Lucetta walked through the door just as Danny and I were getting ready for school. She looked like that expression: like she'd been run over by a truck. Only maybe it wasn't a truck; maybe it was more like a Chevy Impala. Both her arms were bruised, and the side of her face was swollen. She had a split lip too.

"I'm tired, boys," she said, turning sideways so we couldn't see her face. "Y'all get going to school. I'm going to take me a nap."

"What happened?" Danny asked.

"I fell, is all."

"You *fell*?" I could tell he was close to bursting into tears.

"Miss Lu had a little too much to drink," she said.

"Are you all right?"

"Leave me alone, and get yourselves off to school," she said. "I'll be all right."

I could tell by the hard tone in her voice that she meant business, but Danny just stood there, like his engine had stalled out but good.

"You heard me, little man," she said. "Get going now."

"Let's *go*," I said, grabbing Danny by the top of his sleeve and pulling him toward the door. But again, he wouldn't budge. "But Miss Lucetta . . ." he began to say.

"Lookit," she finally said. "Y'all already know I'm no saint. I like to party, is all. But like I say, this isn't some big deal. Y'all go on to school, and when you get back you wake me on up, hear? You just be sure to knock on that door first in case I'm in my birthday suit. And after y'all wake me up, we'll go on down to that bank and get some money for y'all. How does that sound?"

"You'll still be here?" Danny said, and I couldn't tell if he wanted her to stay or not. But one way or the other, he allowed me to drag him on out the door. The last thing I saw before we marched out into the morning was Lucetta limping into Mamma's room.

Mondays were always kind of rough at school—it was as if over the weekend everyone had been drinking some kind of high-energy juice that made them act even crazier than usual—but that Monday was one of the roughest. During first period, two kids got into a fight with razors, one of them slashing the other on the arm, and both of them ending up bleeding all over the place. The school went on instant lockdown until the paramedics came to take the boys away. Then Mrs. Jessup got on the loudspeaker system and said that if there was so much as a hint of trouble the whole school would go on lockdown again, no questions asked. By the time that mess was over it was almost noon, and my stomach was doing flip-flops. Math was its usual torture session, with kids busting out all over the place making the stupidest jokes you ever did hear—*sure would like some of that pi for myself, maybe apple pie*, that kind of thing. All the while, in front of me, Kia was twirling her hair behind her ears and not even noticing that I was sitting right behind her, thinking about doing all kinds of X-rated things with her and worrying about my privates giving me away and then trying to stomp down on my own thoughts. While I was busy trying to shut my mind off, I completely lost track of what the teacher was teaching. In the middle of that, wouldn't you know it, she called on me. When I finally tuned in enough to know she was calling on me, I looked up to see a math problem on the blackboard that may as well have been written in Chinese. "Well, James?" Ms. Baker said as I stared like a dead fish. Everyone laughed like they'd never experienced anything so funny before in their entire lives.

"Kia?" Ms. Baker said. "You want to try?"

"Remove parentheses by multiplying factors, use exponent rules to remove parentheses in terms with exponents, combine like terms by adding coefficients," she said. "Which makes . . . sixty-two."

"There you have it," Ms. Baker said.

Unlike some girls, Kia didn't just understand math, she was smart at it and didn't mind that people knew it. Didn't matter what the teacher threw at us, she got it. Whereas even when my mind wasn't making dirty movies, math was hard for me, all those ratios and divisibility, numbers stacked on symbols stacked on numbers and not lining up right. But then again, I never had been a math whiz, not like Kia, not to mention Gabriel.

I liked English best, especially if the teacher chose something good to read, and not something horrible and depressing like *Lord of the Flies*. Thank goodness we were done with the dreadful *Flies.* Now we were reading *The Adventures of Tom Sawyer*, which frankly wasn't exactly a laugh riot. The teacher kept talking about how it was about teenagers not all that different from us, but I didn't see how a story about a bunch of hick boys who live in some little town in the middle of nowhere a million years ago had much to do with kids at Springs City High in Crystal Springs, Louisiana. But at least it wasn't *Lord of the Disgusting Flies.*

Once class was let out, what everyone talked about was the two kids who had slashed each other. The rumors were flying. Then, right as things were calming down some, the power shut off, and we had to go on lockdown again, just in case. Even with the teachers cranking open all the windows, it was hot in that school, smelling like chalk dust and BO.

Later that day, who should come easing around the

corner but Gabriel, whose grin was even bigger than usual. He clapped me on the back and, in a voice so loud you'd think he was hoping that people on the other side of town could hear him too, asked me how things were going with Lucetta. "She going to be doing some *good* homemade cooking for y'all," he said. "Yes, indeed." I gave him a look that was supposed to mean *shut up*, but he kept on talking. "You be all right now, my man," he said. "No foster care for you and little scooter, no sir. You and little scooter, you my true-blue bros. Things are on track now. Things are being done with true organizational excellence."

Only, of course, they weren't. Just for starters, I was so worried about what Lucetta might be doing inside our house while we were gone that even without the X-rated films that kept cropping up in my mind, it wasn't just math I couldn't do; I couldn't concentrate on any of my classes. In history, when the teacher asked me to name the most important French colonies, I couldn't come up with even one. In bio, I forgot the difference between prokaryotic and eukaryotic cells. At lunch time, the lunch ladies saw me stuffing extra tater tots into my booksack and made me dump them all out. After that, I couldn't even manage to swipe an extra piece of bread. All I could do, all day long, was worry about whether Lucetta had burned the house down with one of her cigarettes or stolen Mamma's jewelry or invited her low-life friends over.

I just sat there all day, picturing the whole scene in my head—how Lucetta and her friends would steal everything in the house, including Mamma's jewelry and her beautiful glass birds, leaving us with nothing left of her at all. As I sat imagining coming home to find the rooms stripped bare and no sign of Lucetta, I could feel the hot tears welling up in my throat and nose. Right then, I knew I had to do something.

What I had to do was get into Mamma's room, take Mamma's jewelry box, and hide it, good. Because if there was one thing I don't think I could stand, it would have been the sight of Lucetta wearing Mamma's heart necklace. Seeing her in Mamma's pink bathrobe was bad enough. But if she started wearing her jewelry—or worse, if she pawned it? I couldn't even think about it. The one thing I knew for sure is that I'd have to be careful, waiting for a time when Lucetta was out of the house, because if I tried to go into Mamma's room when Lucetta was home all hell would break loose.

"Man, didn't I tell you?" Gabriel said later, slinging his big old meat-paws over my shoulder and knocking me into the lockers while he was at it. "Things are going to be smooth sailing, from now on in." Seeing as I had a shooting pain in my stomach that was so bad that I was nearly doubled over, it was hard for me resist cussing him out, especially as Gabriel, being Gabriel, was oblivious. "What you looking like that for? You've just got to have some faith, is all. You've got to have some trust in the adjusted engineering system. Because me? I know about things being tough. If it hadn't been for Auntie, who knows what would have happened to me? I might be dead for now, and I'm not lying. It isn't easy being an orphan, and that's the God's honest truth. But you and me, and little scooter too, that's just what we are, and there's no changing it."

"And your point is?" I managed to say. "And keep your voice down. People can hear."

"Just that I know you still be missing your mom and dad," Gabriel whispered. "'Course you are. That was rough—*rough*— what happened to y'all. But you'll pull through. You'll see. Just got to keep on keeping on. You just got to make an executive decision and stick to it. Just got to *decide* to keep on keeping on. That's how me and Auntie are doing it." By now his voice was loud again, but at least the bell had rung and most kids were hurrying to get to class on time, leaving us with most of the hall to ourselves.

"How are you even related to your auntie?" I asked. "Is she on your mother's side or your father's? Or what? Because you sure don't look like her."

"True!" Gabriel said, patting his big stomach. It was a mystery, how those two went together. Where we lived, all kinds of people lived together, and mainly no one bothered with them unless there was some reason you had to. Otherwise, you didn't want to go poking your nose into someone else's business. At least I knew who my kin were and how I was related to them—even if, except for Lila, they were all dead. I was thinking along like this when Gabriel must have read my mind.

"Matter of fact, Auntie's taking me to New Orleans for Christmas," he said. "We're going to go visit us some folks."

"You got family in New Orleans?"

"Auntie's been saving up and saving up," he said, ignoring the question. "I haven't been back since I was a little kid in foster care there, but she said it isn't going to be like that, it's going to be a special trip, just her and me, and we're going to go to the zoo and see the sights, go out to dinner, stay at a hotel, everything."

New Orleans wasn't far away, and I knew lots of kids who had gone, including me and Danny. Still, I felt a little flicker of envy working its way through my chest and then getting stuck in my throat. I knew I wasn't going to be going to New Orleans, or anywhere, anytime soon. And as for staying at a hotel? I couldn't even imagine.

When I got home, the house was quiet. Mamma's door was closed. I tiptoed over and cracked it open, just enough to see inside; Lucetta was on the bed, sleeping in the same clothes she'd worn when she'd left the day before. The whole house smelled like cigarette smoke, but otherwise everything was the same. *That damn Earl!* the birds chirped as I poked around, making sure I hadn't missed anything. *I miss my baby!*

Just then the mail slapped through the front door slot. We never got anything but bills and ads, so I was surprised when I saw a postcard with a picture of a beach on the front. "Welcome to Sunny Santa Monica!" it said. I couldn't figure out for the life of me who could have sent the postcard, but then I flipped it over.

Dear Mamma, Daddy, Grandma, James, and Danny,

I am writing to you from my home in California. It is beautiful here, and Zip and I are very happy. I know I haven't written in a very long time, and I am truly sorry. But I just wanted you to know that we made it to the west coast and everything is fine.

Love,

Lila

I stared and stared at her handwriting, reading and rereading what she'd written, until all the words blurred together and I couldn't make sense of it at all. Meantime, the birds were talking up a storm. *I love you! College boy! Damn that Earl!* Suddenly I had such a pain in my stomach that I had to run to the bathroom. It was like my entire insides wanted to come out.

When Danny got home from school a little while later, he didn't even say hi. Instead, he pulled a plastic bag with something in it out of his booksack, knocked on Lucetta's door, and, when she said it was all right, went inside. It was like I wasn't even there. When I went to see what was going on, I felt even worse. Danny was sitting up on the bed right next to her, just like both of us used to do with Mamma when we were little. Through the crack in the door, I listened in: Lucetta was saying stuff like "Mind that you talk respectful to your teachers," and he was saying stuff like "Don't your people know where you're at?" The two of them were talking like they'd been best friends for years. He kept asking her if she was sure she was all right, and she kept telling him that now that she'd had her beauty sleep, she was as good as new. "I can be clumsy at times, child, and don't you know it!" she said. "Especially when I've been drinking. Lord have mercy. Sometimes I just can't stop myself. I know it's a sin, but Jesus is good, child."

A minute later, Danny reached into the plastic bag he'd brought in and said he had something he wanted to give her. "A gift?" she said. "For me? Aren't you thoughtful!"

"I don't know," he said, putting a pink-and-yellow lump onto the blanket between them and explaining that it was supposed to be bird. "I made it in art class," he said. To me it looked like a glob of old oatmeal painted pink and yellow, but the way Lucetta was looking at it, you'd think it was the world's biggest diamond. "I made it for Mamma," he whispered. Then he said, "You can have it if you want it." The next thing I know Lucetta's going on and on about how fine the bird was and how she'd keep it by the bed so she could look at it first thing in the morning when she woke up.

"You're a sweet boy, is exactly what you are," she said. "And this is just about the finest present I ever have had."

"You really like it?"

13

HOW WE GOT BY

The miracle was that Gabriel's master plan worked. Sort of.
We had a routine: Every Monday, when we got home from
school, all three of us would go down to the bank with Lucetta.
She'd cash a check for a hundred dollars, using Mamma's
driver's license and cash card for identification. Then she'd
pocket some for herself—Lucetta said that it was the cost of
doing business—and give us the rest. Meanwhile, I did the
accounts. Once Gabriel showed me how to do it, it wasn't
any big deal. Every month, the bank would send us a statement that showed how much money we'd taken out and how
much was left. I'd check the statement, check the bankbook,
and then put everything away, nice and neat, in a box that
I shoved under the bed. Even though I didn't think Lucetta
had any way of getting into our account without our being
with her, I didn't want to take chances. Which is why I kept
hold of Mamma's driver's license and cash card, too, and why
I hid the statements good. And as far as trying to find out

what Mamma's PIN number was? Forget it, because as much as we started liking Lucetta, especially Danny, even he knew that if she got hold of that PIN number, that would be it; we'd be wiped out for good. We couldn't be too careful, not when Lucetta was living with us, not when it came to cash money, anyhow.

Which was the other thing: we never did let Lucetta go near Mamma's checkbook except on Mondays, when we all went down to the bank together. The rest of the time, I personally kept the checkbook not just under my pillow, but *inside* it. I'd made a small slit in the fabric for just that purpose, and with the pillow case on top of it, you'd never find out.

I'd gone ahead and found the perfect hiding place for Mamma's jewelry box, too, inside that old broken-down washing machine in the shed out back. Only I didn't just shove it in there where you could see it if you happened to open the lid. What I did was put the jewelry box inside a shoebox and then put the shoebox inside an empty box of laundry detergent, and then I hid the detergent box inside the washing machine. I even put a piece of tape over the lid of the box of detergent, so I could see, first thing, if anyone had been fooling with it. Chances were that no one was going to be looking in that rusty machine to begin with, but just in case, that's where the camouflage came in. Even so, when Lucetta was napping or going about her business somewhere else, I checked it, to make sure. I checked to make sure that the box was taped shut, just like I'd left it. Sometimes I even picked it up and shook it. Sure enough, I'd hear the *clink clink clink* of Mamma's jewelry.

That washing machine was so old it was never going to work again. Even Lucetta said that we'd just have to make do with the laundromat because fixing up that junky old machine was going to cost too much money and buying a new one was downright impossible, so I knew she wasn't going to mess with it. We'd even gone ahead and put the hamper inside, in the hall next to Grandma's old room. It was Lucetta's idea, because when it came to dirty clothes, she was a neat freak. Danny and I did the laundry every Sunday, hauling it down to the Washeteria on Main Street, everything in one big load because it cost less money that way. And once the weather finally started turning, it was nice in there, because we could lie right on top of those steaming machines and warm up.

I was paying the bills too. Keeping track of the bills wasn't nothing once I got the hang of it. And after practicing a few times, I could forge Mamma's signature pretty well.

Even though she hardly ever cooked, Lucetta fussed at us to eat right, telling us to buy fruit and yogurt and eggs and things like that and to stay away from things that came pre-pared in the box. But when she did cook, it was like we were a real family, sitting over a dinner of meatloaf or baked ham with sweet potatoes, with big glasses of lemonade and fruit pie for dessert. The main thing of it was that Danny and I had money to buy food again, and I cooked for us as best I could. At least I didn't have to hunt through dumpsters any-more. And as for Danny, he finally stopped complaining about being hungry. Plus, he was happier. After school, if Lucetta was home, he'd barge right on in on her to talk. Even though I didn't like to admit it, even I had to concede that she listened. She wasn't pretending to, either. You could tell right away that she didn't mind, that she downright liked Danny—liked having him around, liked having him lie next to her on the big bed and tell her about school. "You make me smile, with all that sugar of yours," she'd say, throwing her arms around him and letting him lie with his head on her lap. "Sweet as sugar and then some."

But the truth was that Lucetta hardly did anything at all. Mainly she slept. When she wasn't sleeping, she was watching TV. And if she wasn't doing either of those two things, she wasn't home much at all.

Even so, Danny and me, we got so used to Lucetta's ways—her talking to herself and her napping and the way she'd stand in front of the birdcage telling Cher and Sonny about people she knew—that when she wasn't home when we got back from school we worried something awful. Her swollen lip had cleared up just fine, but we always worried that there'd be a next time. If she didn't call to tell us when she was coming back, Danny would freak. And it wasn't like she couldn't call; I made sure to pay the phone company nice and regular, every month, because with Danny being the age he was it was important to have a phone.

"You got that right," Lucetta said. "I've got to have a phone in order to conduct my business too."

"What business?" Danny said.

"The mind-your-own-business business," she said.

Then she'd go out—and she wouldn't call, not even once, no matter how many times we begged her to let us know where she was and when she was coming back.

"What does she do when she isn't here?" Danny said one night, when the two of us were huddled up together in the little room in back. "Do you think she has a job?"

"If she does have a job, it wouldn't be the regular kind," I said.

"What kind then?"

"I don't know myself," I said. "Some kind of mess that we don't need to know about."

"But *James*," he said, "what if she gets in trouble? What if she gets hurt?"

"Well, yeah," I said. "She isn't hurt, and she isn't in trouble. All right? Stop worrying." But of course I was worried myself, so worried that pretty much every day I got a stomachache so bad that it was all I could do to crawl from one class to another. But because I was one of those kids that no one noticed, no one noticed. Not Gabriel. Not my teachers. Not Danny. And certainly not Kia.

Kia! That girl got prettier and prettier, and smarter and smarter, every time I saw her. There wasn't nothing about algebra that she didn't understand; she could do integers, metrics, square roots, polynomials, exponents, signed numbers, coefficients, everything. Aside from Gabriel, she was the smartest person in math I knew. Sitting behind her day after day felt like a combination of being in a torture chamber and being in the kind of dream you don't want to wake up from.

In November, my birthday rolled round, right on schedule. Danny gave me a pair of socks and Lucetta sang the "Happy Birthday" song. But that was it. Gabriel was getting so caught up in going to New Orleans over Christmas vacation that, even though I'd mentioned it to him a half dozen times, he didn't even remember it was my birthday, which was weird, because Gabriel remembered everything about everything. The other thing that was weird was that there were days when I hardly saw Gabriel at all. Then, of course, when I *did* see him, he'd be all over me, talking a mile a minute in that embarrassing way he had. "Yo, man," was all he said when I saw him a day or two after my birthday. "Getting to be a regular big guy now." I didn't know if he meant my birthday or my height; at last I'd started to grow. The way I could tell was that suddenly my pants didn't quite reach down long enough. That, plus my shoes were getting tight. One night I hit a fever and started sweating all over, and the next morning, I was taller than Lucetta. I wouldn't have believed it myself, but we stood back-to-back and it was true. "Golly all," she said. "That fever of yours was nothing but your bones growing so fast they done heated you up."

"My sheets are soaked through, I sweated so much," I said.

"What'd you want me to do about it?"

I didn't tell her that, seeing as I had to get to school, I was hoping that she'd put clean sheets on like Mamma would have. But she must have known what I was thinking, because before I even had a chance to adjust to my new height, she said, "I like helping you boys out, but you know, and I done told you and told you, if I'd a wanted to be a maid, I would have gone and been a maid. But I'm not your maid, and you two boys are plenty big to fix your own beds good." She lit a cigarette. "What we need around here is our own dang washing machine, for sure. But we can't afford it. Lord knows I don't make much money, but even when I do well, I just can't seem to hold on to it. That's life, I guess." When Danny asked her what she did to make money, she said, "Never you mind," letting smoke out of her nose in two long gray streams, like a dragon. I didn't know what she meant either, but I figured it had something to do with something that wasn't legal—drugs maybe, because it wasn't like Crystal Springs didn't have its drug dealers, and worse.

Then Thanksgiving came, and Lucetta surprised us by cooking. She made a roast chicken, and we sat down together, holding hands while Danny made the blessing: "Dear Heavenly Father, for this food which upon us you bestow we are eternally grateful in Jesus's name, amen."

"Amen," Lucetta said.

Amen! Jesus! College man! Stop it, Earl!

"Quiet, you birds," Lucetta hissed.

God damn! Stop it, Earl! Amen! This is it?

"Why are the birds talking about Earl like that?" Danny said.

"Haven't I told you to keep your nose where it belongs?"

"But Miss Lu!"

"Don't ruin the holiday, little thing," she said.

Stop it, Earl, stop it, stop it!

"But what do the birds know that we don't?"

He had a point, but Lucetta just smiled. "These birds of y'all's," she said, "they sure are crazy."

14

MORE POSTCARDS

Not long after Thanksgiving, another postcard came from Lila. This one had a picture of the Hollywood Hills on it. I knew because of the Hollywood sign, all lit up, which I'd seen on TV. On the back, over the stamp, was the postmark: LA.

Just wanted to let you know that things are fine, only I sure have been missing you. How's my little brother Danny doing? He must be a big boy by now. Tell bro James not to read too much! I'm working in showbiz!

Love,
Lila

As if that helped anything. Lila had been gone so long that I could hardly remember her. She'd been gone so long that she didn't know that everyone had upped and died. She'd been gone so long that, except for Danny and me, no one even remembered her name. Suddenly, I hated Lila. I hated her with every bone in my body and every cell in my blood. My lungs hated her, and my intestines, and my pancreas, and my liver. My stomach balled up like it was filled with clay.

"What's that, James?" It was Lucetta, coming up behind me wearing a light-blue silk kerchief on her head and white fluffy slippers on her feet. Mamma's kerchief; Mamma's fluffy slippers. I don't know why, but seeing Lucetta wearing Mamma's things, even though Mamma couldn't use them anymore, made me even angrier, more filled with hatred.

"Nothing," I said.

"Let me see it," she said, swiping the postcard from me before I had a chance to protest. As she leaned in, I could smell the cigarette smoke on her breath mingling with bath soap and powder. Her skin smelled warm and her breath smelled sour and her clothes smelled like Mamma.

"Who's Lila?" she asked.

"My cousin."

"She says you boys are her brothers."

"But we aren't."

"I thought you said you didn't have any other kin."

"Don't. Lila ran away, back when I was just a little kid myself. Went all the way to California. She's *gone*."

"You don't know where she's at?"

"Like I said, she's gone to California."

"Lila, huh?"

"That's her name."

Lucetta just looked at me for a while with her big, soft, liquid, yellow-brown eyes. "I used to know a girl by the name of Lila," she muttered. "Lila Lee or some such."

The birds must have liked the sound of that, because they immediately began singing: *Lila Lee! Lila Lee!*

"You okay, James?" she said. "You look downright—are you getting sick?"

"I'm fine," I said, even though I wasn't. Lila's full name was Lila Lisa Moore. But *Lila Lee* was what Mamma and Daddy sometimes called her, when they were teasing.

"You don't look fine."

"So?"

"So if you don't feel good, come and get me, hear? A boy shouldn't be getting sick and not telling no one about it."

Then she turned on her heel and went back to the bedroom. Lord knows why she was so tired all the time, but that woman sure did sleep a lot.

After that, the postcards kept on coming—almost one a day. Always with pictures of sunny California on the front: mountains, ocean, beaches, Mickey Mouse, movie stars. All sorts of things that we don't have in Louisiana. And each time, if she was home when the mail came slapping through the front door slot, Lucetta would come padding over to take a look. The messages were always pretty much the same too:

Just wanted to tell you that things are fine and I miss y'all.

Love,

Lila

In other words, nothing. I tore the postcards up. Merely looking at them made my stomach hurt so much it was like someone had come along and plunged a knife into my guts. Plus, I didn't want Danny getting his hands on those postcards and getting his hopes up. Because as much as *I* didn't remember Lila, Danny didn't remember Lila even more. I figured she must be twenty-three or twenty-four by now, maybe older. Stupid, selfish Lila was living the good life in Los Angeles, working, with her own apartment and a beach in her front yard. Sunshine, movie stars, dinner out every day of the week.

Gabriel didn't know about the postcards either, because I figured if I told him about them, he might start thinking up some new scheme in his mind. But as it happened, he was so worked up about his trip to New Orleans with his auntie that that's all he could think about anyway. Since Lucetta had moved in, we'd seen less and less of Gabriel, which in some ways was a relief. I'd hardly ever see him around the neighborhood at all, but when I saw him in school, he'd be like "Twenty-one more days, Jack, until vacation in the Big ol' Easy." What I'm saying is for Gabriel, New Orleans was the Promised Land. He just couldn't *wait* for Christmas vacation to come rolling around. All he talked about on the way to school was New Orleans. All he talked about on the way home was New Orleans. He talked so much about New Orleans that I began to feel like I lived there myself. It was pure Gabriel: once he got onto a subject, dude just wouldn't let it go. It was like he was missing a piece of his brain, the piece most people have that let them know when to stop talking. But the whole thing was stupid, too, because who cared about his stupid old trip to New Orleans? It wasn't like he was going to China. He was just going down I-10 for a spell.

"You know what they got there, don't you?" he said, shoving Doritos into his mouth. It had cooled off good by now and was cold at night, so walking to school carrying tons of books in my booksack wasn't the torture it had been. "First off, they've got the world's most beautiful women."

As if, I thought.

"Second, they got the best food. Restaurants serving every kind of good thing you can imagine—crawfish coming out of your ears, and steak, and oh man! The desserts! We're gonna be eating *good*. Auntie's been saving up, yes indeed. Also, the zoo, like I said. We're going to see the lions and the alligators and the monkeys. And, son, did I tell you? They've got all kinds of wild-looking birds there, too, big old birds that would make your little birdies seem like little old moths in comparison."

"Yeah," I said. "Whatever."

"Auntie's been working extra. Making almost ten dollars an hour, but you times that by overtime and then put it toward six nights at a hotel, plus dinner, plus extras, plus bus. That comes to almost a thousand dollars, I'd say, let's see . . ." He scratched his head, the way he did when he was figuring. "Something like nine hundred and twenty, nine hundred and thirty dollars. I tell you, Auntie's been working hard, and you know, I've been helping out."

This was news to me. No wonder he hadn't been around much. As if reading my mind, he started filling in the blanks.

"Just yard work and stuff. Whatever I can get. Plus helping out washing cars. I've been working at the car wash on Liberty. Trying to help Auntie, best as I can. Did I tell you we're staying at a hotel, the River Edge hotel? That's just what it's called— River Edge." And on and on he'd go, until I couldn't stand his babbling anymore. *His* job at the car wash. *His* auntie. *His* plans for Christmas. It seemed that he'd plain old forgotten about Danny and me.

A few days later, things got worse. Lucetta wasn't home when I got home, but that wasn't unusual. She wasn't there when Danny got home, either, but that, too, was no big deal, as by then we were used to her ways. We started to worry when ten o'clock rolled around and she hadn't shown up. When I got up to take a pee in the middle of the night, she still wasn't home. And in the early morning, when I woke up from a bad dream—all manner of dogs chewing at my fingers and toes—I got up to check, only to find that she was still out. I had a bad feeling that maybe, this time, she'd upped and left—taking Mamma's jewelry with her, and who knows what else.

But in the morning when I went out back to check, the detergent box was just where I'd left it, taped up and heavy with the jinglejangle of Mamma's jewelry, inside that empty broken-down old washing machine. The TV was in its usual place too. Still, I was worried. She didn't come home the next day either, or that night. Danny and I lay there in our beds in the back room, staring up at the ceiling and hoping nothing bad had happened.

The thing is, I could have moved back into Grandma's room, like before. But even after Lucetta came to live with us, I really didn't want to leave Danny by himself, not even at night when he was asleep. I don't know why. Even Danny wanted me to move on out, but I just had a feeling, so I stayed. I stayed, dreaming about dogs going after me, chewing my fingers and toes, biting into my brains.

There was no Lucetta when we got up for school the next day, either. We couldn't even imagine where she was or why she hadn't called. Finally, though, just as Danny and I were having breakfast, we heard the door bang open, and there she was. Or at least we *thought* it was Lucetta. It was hard to tell who was under the mess of bruises and sores that came dragging into our living room. Both her eyes were so busted up that her skin was more blue than beige. Her lower lip was bloody and oozing, and she dragged one leg behind the other, lurching like a zombie. She smelled bad too. Smelled like vomit, cigarettes, beer, and something else—something so bad I couldn't even name it.

"Miss Lu!" Danny called, getting up so quickly that he spilled his bowl of Frosted Flakes all over the floor.

She didn't reply.

"Miss Lu! We gotta get you a doctor."

"No doctor," she muttered, limping through the door to her bedroom.

"But you're hurt," Danny said.

"I've been worse."

And with that, she half collapsed, half dove for the bed, where she rolled over to one side, pulling her feet up behind her. "Miss Lu!" Danny cried, getting up onto the bed next to her. "What happened? Miss Lu?"

When she didn't answer, he turned to me. "Is she going to die, James?"

"I'm not gonna die," she managed to whisper, but any fool could see that she wasn't in any shape to take care of herself, either. We didn't know what to do, but we did it anyway. Danny and I pulled off her shoes and covered her with blankets, brought her water and a wet washcloth, and helped clean her face. As we worked, she fell asleep, but then she woke up again, opening her eyes. "Go to school, y'all," she said in a croaky whisper.

Danny and I looked at each other.

"Go," she said, letting her lids fall shut again.

"But Miss Lucetta!" Danny was beginning to cry; I could always tell, because even before the tears formed in his eyes, his pupils grew to be the size of pennies, so that his eyes were almost entirely black in the center, with hardly any brown, and his lower lip would quiver some as he clenched his jaw. "What if you die?"

"No one's going to die," Lucetta said.

"But Miss Lu!"

Finally Lucetta took a deep breath and, speaking in a low, even tone, said, "If you don't go, then I will."

At lunch, I told Gabriel what had happened. I didn't have anyone *else* to tell. Me, I figured Lucetta had some boyfriend somewhere and he beat on her. Maybe he caught her with some other man. Maybe he gave her drugs and she hadn't paid him.

But Gabriel offered up his own theory. "Nah, man," he said. "I don't see it that way. I'm not saying that Lucetta's some kind of angel, because, obviously, if she were we never would have found her down at the Mercy and Grace Center to begin with. But if she were really running with the drug crowd? She would have stolen you blind by now. Instead, you've still got all your stuff, your TV set and everything—because a TV, man, a TV's the easiest thing to steal, make a quick profit, no one bothers with it, and the police don't care. She could have stolen every stick of furniture out of y'all's house by now, is the truth. Don't believe me? Just ask Auntie, because it's the truth."

"Then why she coming home beaten up and stinking to high heaven? This is the second time too. The second time in a month."

"It's alcohol, is what I'm thinking," Gabriel said. "She goes out and drinks until she gets stupid, and then . . . well, yeah, maybe she *does* start taking up with the wrong kind of men. Men who beat her up. But maybe not. Maybe she gets into fights. Auntie's been telling me that, back in the day when she was coming up, girls would get into fights nearly as bad as boys, go at each other until there was blood and broken bones, all manner of ugly and stupid. *Especially* when they'd been partying."

"I don't know," I said. "I'm worried."

"You're eating, aren't you?" Gabriel said. "Things are going okay with Danny? You've got a roof over your head. That's what you have to concentrate on—you two brothers are still together, and not in any foster care mess. Understand the distinction?"

I didn't know what it was about Gabriel that made him so oblivious to things, but there was nothing I could say that would convince him that there was any reason to worry about either Danny and me, or about Lucetta. And like usual, by and by, I started believing him all over again: believing that things were working out and that all Danny and I had to do was stick with the program, keep our heads down and our mouths shut, and one day, we'd be grown and on our own and we'd be able to look back at the hard times and know that, together, we got through.

"Yeah," he was saying, grinning that big grin of his as he helped himself to the cornbread on my plate. "You've got to count your *blessings*, man, not dwell on the *sorrows*. That's what I had to learn myself. You just keep on keeping on, you don't look back, tomorrow is another day. That's what Auntie taught me." And he was going on like that when Mrs. Jessup, the principal, came on up behind us, wearing that mean little smile of hers that meant she had you in her sights. "Gabriel Keyes!" she said.

"What do *you* want?" Gabriel answered before he knew who he was talking to. With that, she let her gaze fall on me, narrowing her eyes as if she knew what we were up to and didn't like it. "That's it, in my office," she said. I almost peed in my pants, but it was Gabriel she wanted, and a minute later, he was following her out through the cafeteria doors, heading to detention, or worse.

15

KIA

In math that day, Kia turned around, looked right at me, and said, "You're James, right?"

I was so startled it was all I could do to nod my head. She knew my name! I tried not to stare. Kia's gold earrings glinted in her ears. She brushed a stray hair out of her mouth.

"Do you have a little brother named Danny?"

I nodded.

"Because your brother? He's in my brother's grade. At Prescott Middle? He's picking on my brother, bad. Picking fights with *everyone*."

"What?" I finally said.

"Your brother is Danny Moore?"

"Danny's picking fights?"

"My brother, Kyle? He's little for his age. He came home yesterday with a swollen eye. He said your brother did it to him."

I didn't know what to say, so I didn't say anything. Instead, I sat there like a lump, feeling the blood beating into my face. Finally, I opened my mouth. "I'll kill him," I said.

"Yeah, well—" Kia was about to say something else, but just then Ms. Baker came in and started rapping on the blackboard, the way she did when she expected us to sit straight and pay attention.

All during class, I couldn't concentrate even a little, but instead kept thinking about Danny picking fights, punching some boy in the eye. Then there was Gabriel. What had mean old Mrs. Jessup wanted? And what if big-mouth old Gabriel had gone and opened his big mouth about me and Danny? But then, I thought, why should he? If he was in trouble with Mrs. Jessup, it would probably be for the usual things, like letting his pants droop down halfway off his butt or juggling donuts in gym class. Meanwhile, even with everything I was worrying over, I couldn't take my eyes off Kia. She answered every question perfectly, and, as she bent over her work, the sunlight shone through her ears. I was fascinated by the back of her ears, the way they glowed pink, like colored glass.

"Kia," I said as the bell rang.

"Yes?"

I wanted to tell her that I'd have a talk with Danny and get the whole thing straightened out. But as I paused to find the right words, she gave me a long, blank look, turned on her heel, and disappeared into the hallway. I felt so stupid that as I followed the other kids out of the classroom, I almost didn't see Mrs. Jessup coming around the corner and nearly crashed into her. "Watch where you're going, young man," she said. I was lucky she didn't give me a detention on the spot. I thought for sure she'd give me another one of her withering looks and remember that I was the loser who hung around Gabriel. Instead, she passed on.

For the first time in a while, Gabriel caught up with me as I was leaving school. "What happened?" I asked.

"What you mean?"

"With Mrs. Jessup?" I said. "You in trouble?"

Gabriel shrugged. "Nah, man. Mrs. Jessup's all right." Then he clammed up—or at least he clammed up about Mrs. Jessup. He wanted to talk about the usual subject: all the great stuff he and his auntie were going to do in New Orleans. Seeing that I'd heard it about twelve times already, it was getting tedious.

It didn't matter what he said or didn't say, though, because all I could really think about was what I was going to tell Danny. The more I thought about it, the more my stomach hurt. Hitting kids? Beating on them? He was going to get his butt kicked in if he kept on like that, and then we'd be in the toilet for real. And what if he denied everything? On the other hand, what did any of it matter if I got home to find that Lucetta had bled to death?

"What's eating you?" Gabriel said, interrupting my thoughts.

"What?"

"You seem grumpy."

"Grumpy?"

"Disturbed. Distressed. Depressed. Disoriented."

"Bye," I said.

"What?"

"I've got to go." We were standing just outside my house, and I couldn't wait even one more moment or I'd have an accident on the sidewalk.

I made it to the bathroom just in time. Even so, I still didn't feel so good. And I felt even worse when, coming out of the bathroom, I heard the sound of Danny yelping like a hyena coming from Mamma/Lucetta's room. I didn't know why, but something about that sound set my teeth on edge.

When I went to investigate, what I found wasn't anything like what I'd imagined, because what I'd imagined was that Danny had come home to find Lucetta dead and gone and plumb lost his mind. Instead, he was sitting up in the bed next to her, the two of them snuggled up like girls at a sleepover party, drinking Coke and watching TV.

"Guess you're feeling better," I said, glancing in the doorway.

"Why shoot, boy," Lucetta said. "Don't say it like that. I told you I'd be okay."

"Well. Yeah. You are."

THE ART OF DUMPSTER DIVING

"And your sweet little brother here. Do you know what he did?" Without waiting for a reply, she went on. "I want to tan his hide anyway, because he skipped school. And you *know* your job is to go to school and study what the teacher teaches you. But this boy? He pretended to go off to school, but he never got there. He came right back. Spent the whole day sitting up with me, telling me stories, bringing me cold drinks. Then he brought the TV on in so I could watch from bed. Shoot, he sure is some kind of sweet kid."

Danny was grinning from ear to ear, blushing.

"But it's not right," I finally said.

"What's not right, James? Your brother is a good boy. Why are you looking at me like that? What's on your mind?"

"Danny's supposed to be in school," I said.

"Yeah, well."

The two of them, giggling, traded glances.

"He's supposed to be in class, learning."

"I can't argue with you, James," Lucetta said. "But just this one time, he played hooky. And all because he wanted to look after me. Don't be all put out by it. You're a good brother, that's for sure. But he's just a little biscuit, this one is. He'll go to school tomorrow, won't you, Danny?"

"Yes, Miss Lu."

"See?"

But I didn't see anything—except my own anger. I was so angry the room swam before me.

"You know some boy by the name of Kyle?" I asked Danny.

"I don't know. Maybe. Know a lot of kids."

"Look at me," I said. "Turn away from that damn TV and look at me."

"You're not my boss."

"Danny," I said. "You and me. We have to have a talk."

"I didn't do anything!" he said.

"You hit him," I said.

"Maybe the boy has to protect himself," Lucetta said. "Ever think about that?"

"What's got into you, Danny?"

"You faggot, James. I done told you. I didn't do *anything*. You got some problem with that?"

"But I heard you did."

"What do I care?"

From the TV came the sound of a laugh track, while from my stomach came the sounds of weird, empty, rattling gurgling.

"Well," Lucetta said to Danny. "Did you or didn't you?"

"I swear," he said. "I never hit no kid."

"You see?" Lucetta said. "He swears he didn't do it. Must be some mix-up." She leaned over to brush some crumbs onto the floor. "Want to join us, James?" she asked. "I know you're a big boy, in high school and all that. But there's room for one more."

Did I? A part of me wanted nothing more than to climb onto that bed with Danny and Lucetta and lean up against the pillows and watch some dumb TV show. But another part of me, the hard, scared, proud part, wanted nothing to do with any of it.

"Can't," I said. "Homework."

After that, things started happening fast—though looking back on all of it, it seems more like it all happened in slow motion. Danny started coming home from school earlier and earlier, sometimes with cuts on his face and hands. Lucetta would cluck over him, clean him up, and let him climb into the bed with her, where they'd watch TV. The principal called, saying she wanted to talk to Mrs. Moore, and I kept saying that she was working overtime, working double shift, working out of town. In other words, I lied. But I didn't know how much longer I could get away with it before she sent someone knocking on our door. Danny didn't seem to care. And Lucetta, for all her talk about how important an education was, seemed happy with the way things were going too. She even took the phone calls herself a couple of times, saying she was babysitting while Mamma was at work while Danny's asthma was acting up. Asthma? Danny didn't have asthma. Sometimes the two of them would spend the day doing nothing but watching TV and eating pizza. Other times they'd nap. Once when I came home from school, I found them having a pillow fight, laughing like crazy while feathers flew through the room. Finally I realized that I'd have to scare some sense into Danny, telling him that the school was sending over a truancy officer. But even that didn't frighten him, leastways not enough for him to go to school steady. It wasn't that he didn't go at all, though. He went enough that the principal stopped calling. But he wasn't learning; any idiot could see that.

Heck, I was barely learning myself, not with everything that was on my mind. At least, in English, we'd finished with stupid Tom Sawyer. Now we were reading *The Natural*, which made me cry. Meanwhile, Gabriel couldn't talk about anything other than New Orleans. "Gawd dang," he'd say, when I saw him in the cafeteria, "this is gonna be the best Christmas ever."

I doubted it.

Just a few days before vacation was set to start, I rounded the corner to our house to see the mailman leaving the neighborhood, an hour or so earlier than usual. When I let myself inside, I found Danny sitting on the sectional, reading a postcard. "It's from Lila," he said, handing it to me. Glancing at it, I saw that it was just more of the same, a whole lot of nothing.

But for Danny, it was like he'd swallowed a curiosity pill. He'd never so much as mentioned her name to me in all this time, but now he was talking a mile a minute, asking questions. Where did she live, and why had she run off? Why couldn't we call her? Maybe if we found her, she'd come back. He asked me why I hadn't tried to find her and whether she'd written before, and when Lucetta came out of the bedroom and said, "Yes, she wrote," he went downright crazy.

"She already wrote to us, and you never told me? Where she at? We got to find her! What's wrong with you? You call yourself my brother? What kind of brother doesn't let his own brother know about something like this? Why didn't you tell me? Where she at?"

I told him that I didn't know, but he kept at me, until he'd worked himself up into a rage and started hammering at me—with his fists. But since I'd started growing some, I was able to pin his hands behind him pretty fast. "That's enough," I said.

"Get out of my face!"

"This is the kind of thing you get up to at school?"

"Asswipe!"

"This is why you're coming home with cuts all over your hands? Picking fights?"

"Liar," he said. "Butthole."

"You just calm yourself now."

"Where you put her other letters?" he screamed.

"Threw 'em out."

"Just like you threw Mamma out?"

"You've gone crazy."

"If you didn't kill her yourself, then how come you never told me where you done PUT HER!" And he went loco nuts all over again, butting me with his head and trying to take bites out of my shirt. Even though I was bigger than him, he was fast. Strong too. When he bit me, I didn't have a choice. His teeth were tearing into me. I kicked him in the stomach until he let go.

"Dickhead!" he screamed, collapsing into a heap on the floor. "WHERE IS SHE?" He just lay there for a while, looking at me with eyes smoky with disgust. I didn't know if he was talking about Lila or about Mamma, but either way, I couldn't answer.

Not for one second had I stopped thinking about where we'd put Mamma. Not for one second had I stopped worrying about it either. All this time, I'd been doing my best not to go anywhere near that raggedy old house. Just the thought of it sent waves of panic up my spine.

People who don't live down our way don't realize how hot it is and how long the hot lasts. But it was December, and it was finally cooling off for real. We opened the windows at night to let the breeze in, and it was chilly enough to sleep under blankets.

It was so nice out, the trek home from school would have been pleasant if Gabriel hadn't been going on and on about New Orleans. I'd just walked in the door after enduring another round of him counting down the days until his big trip—when Lila called.

"Who's this?" she said.

"Who's this?"

There was a pause. "This is Lila."

I was silent, hoping that Danny hadn't heard. Lucetta was asleep, I was pretty sure; she'd gone back to her old ways, going out at night, coming home before dawn, and sleeping most of the day. The birds were singing: *Lord, have mercy! College boy! Stop it, Earl! Stop it! Lord, have mercy! Pretty bird! I love you!*

"Lila," I said.

"Is this Daddy?"

"James."

"James," she said. "You sound so grown-up."

"What do you want?"

"Let me talk to Mamma. Please. Is Mamma home?"

"No."

"How about Daddy?"

"He's not available."

"Grandma?"

"Gone out."

I didn't know why I was doing her like that, but suddenly I was so angry, it was all I *could* do. "James?" she said, her voice pitched low. "James. This is serious. I've got to talk to Mamma. It's urgent."

"I done told you already. Mamma's not here."

"When will she be back?"

For a second, I thought about slamming the phone down. How dare she? But then something inside me collapsed, and out it came, the truth.

"Never."

"James?" It wasn't even a whisper, but more of a breath. "What are you talking about, James?"

"She's dead. They're all dead. Mamma. Daddy. Grandma. Dead. Mamma was the last to go."

"Look, James," she said, hissing. "Don't mess with me like that. I know I've been gone a long time."

"Years."

"And I know I shouldn't have done like I did, but . . ."

I waited.

"I've got to go," she said, and just like that, she hung up.

I didn't know that you could call the phone company and have them trace incoming calls, but even if I *had* known I'm not sure I would have done it. The fact of the matter is, I didn't know what to do about anything. I didn't know what to do about Danny. I didn't know what to do about Lila. I didn't even know what to do about me. I was sixteen, almost halfway through high school. I'd finally begun to grow, but I was still shorter than most of the girls, and my legs and arms were as skinny as ever. My voice came out in squeaks and squawks. I sounded like one of Mamma's birds. My stomach hurt all the time, and along with my bad stomach, my breath had turned sour. I could smell it myself. I dreaded going to sleep, because half the time I woke up screaming from a nightmare about dogs and the other half I woke up with my hands on Danny because I was dreaming about Kia. Meantime, in math class, Kia just kept looking prettier and prettier. But ever since she'd told me that Danny had been beating up on her brother, I could barely work up the courage to look at her.

One day, however, she swiveled around in her chair, and just like that, she said, "Are you some kind of orphan?"

I was so startled I could barely stammer out that I didn't know what she meant.

"The thing is?" she said. "My brother's been talking, and he said that your brother claims he's an orphan. My brother says your brother's going around telling everyone that he lives alone with you and that you're starving to death."

"My brother's crazy," I said.

With that, Kia shrugged and turned back around. But me? I had broken out in a sweat all over my body and could barely hear the teacher for the pounding in my ears. If Danny was telling Kia's brother, and Kia's brother was telling Kia, then who else knew? With rumors flying the way they did in our school, and Gabriel with his big mouth, it was only a matter of time until mean old Mrs. Jessup would be calling me into her office. And then? I didn't even want to think about it. All

I knew was that if Danny kept talking, I'd end up in JV prison, or worse.

That afternoon, when I got home to find that Danny had once again skipped school, I did something I'd never done before—I hit him. I really hit him, on purpose, with my fists, and kept at it until he cried and Lucetta, who had dragged herself up out of the bed, was hollering and pulling me off him. "What's gotten into you, James? Are you crazy? Leave this child alone! What's he ever done to you?"

It wasn't until Danny was sniffling on Lucetta's lap and I was crumpled, in shame, on the far end of the sectional, that I heard the birds calling to each other in their singsong, birdy voices: *Stop it, Earl! Are you crazy? Stop it!*

It was almost Christmas.

16

CHRISTMAS VACATION

On Christmas morning, Danny and I woke up to find that Lucetta was gone, along with Mamma's collection of glass birds. Not a bird was left—not the light-blue one with the green eyes, not the clear one with gold speckles, not the black one that looked like it was filled with ink. The only good news was that Cher and Sonny hadn't been touched, though they weren't much help, either, not with all their chirping and complaining: *Help me, Jesus! Pretty bird! Stop it, y'all! Pretty pretty!* There wasn't anyone I could go to for help, either. If I called the police, they'd come and bust me and Danny up, and Gabriel and his auntie had gone to New Orleans.

"Shoot," Danny said, scratching his butt.

We still had enough money, though—or at least I thought we did. But when I went to check the account to make double-sure, the total was less than I had thought—*a lot less.*

Which could only mean one thing: Lucetta. I couldn't figure out how she'd done it. All I knew was that, somehow, she had. Thank goodness I'd put Mamma's jewelry away. Because if worse came to worst . . . .

I didn't want to sell Mamma's things, not for anything. Kia wore gold hoops in her ears and a gold necklace with a cross on it around her neck. Maybe one day I'd give her one of Mamma's rings . . . but what was I thinking? I was still a shrimp, and Kia didn't even talk to me except to ask me things that no one should have to ask.

"You think she stole them?" Danny said.

"Probably."

"Why would she go do that?" he said, whimpering a little.

"I don't know," I said, except I did. Whatever her business was, when she wasn't sleeping in Mamma's bed or hanging out with Danny, Lucetta was bad news, such bad news that she was probably out selling Mamma's collection of birds right now and using the money she got for them for drugs.

"But she loves those birds," Danny said.

"Even so. The birds are gone."

"But she wouldn't steal from us, James. She *couldn't*."

I didn't fully believe it myself. But then, in a sickening inner crunch inside my gut, I understood that not only had she stolen from us, but that she'd probably been stealing from us all along—and I don't mean just the cash money that she skimmed off the top of the weekly allowance we got from the bank.

Just to be on the safe side, I went back out to the shed to make sure that Mamma's jewelry was where I'd hidden it. As always, after I checked to make sure that the tape hadn't been torn, I gave that old detergent box a shake. Hearing Mamma's rings and things rattling around inside her jewelry box, I let out a big old sigh and returned to the house.

"Merry Christmas," I told Danny, who was still just standing there, puzzled. He was wearing the Christmas PJ's—red flannels with a design of prancing reindeer—that he'd gotten the year before, and hugging Bow-Wow to his chest.

"Damn," he said.

At least she hadn't taken the presents or the little plant that we'd put in the corner, the one we'd chosen special because it smelled a little bit like pine. But it wasn't like Christmas was a whole lot of merry, either. Danny opened my present to him: a Saints jersey. Then I opened his to me: a Walkman, brand-new and still wrapped in its original casing. Where he'd gotten the money to buy it was anyone's guess. A few days earlier, I would have questioned him about it, but now I was just too low-down and depressed to do anything but say "thank you." He thanked me too. There were presents from Lucetta too—two boxes that she must have placed under the scraggly little bush right before she'd left. They were wrapped in tinfoil, with bright blue and red ribbons. Inside was aftershave for me—which was pretty funny, seeing as I wouldn't need it for years—and for Danny she'd bought a pair of binoculars. There was no note. Danny and I had pooled our little bit of money to get something for Lucetta: a nice, big bottle of perfume that the lady at the Walgreens said was popular. We left it there under the plant.

Danny and I looked at each other, knowing that it would be a long Christmas vacation, with nothing much to do but watch TV and hope that, when Lucetta came back, she'd be in one piece. *If* Lucetta came back, that is.

This time she didn't come back for four full days. Worse, she wasn't alone.

It was midafternoon when she limped into the house. The left side of her face was pink and puffy; her lips were cut; she carried one arm inside the other, like a broken wing; and she moved so slowly, it was as if she was made of glass. Right behind her was a short man with a big belly, a bald head, and a bushy black mustache. Dressed in a suede overcoat, cowboy boots, and blue jeans, he looked at me and Danny with eyes like slits. "Boys," he said, coming in behind Lucetta and very slowly taking off his coat. "Why don't you two just make yourselves scarce for a little while?"

"Who are you?" Danny said.

"The name is Earl." He sat down on the sectional.

"How do you know Lucetta?"

"Go on now, boys," he said.

"But this is our house," Danny said.

Earl cocked his head, the way you see dogs do. "Lu. Make them move."

"He's right," Lucetta muttered, but there was no heat in her voice, no passion. It was like listening to a tape recording of someone talking.

"You heard the lady," Earl said. "Out."

"But Mr. Earl," Danny said, "this is our house."

"I suggest you do as I say."

"What?"

"Go on now, boys," Lucetta said. "Better get a move on. Go on down to the store, get yourselves some ice cream."

"No!" Danny said.

He was standing near the empty cabinet where the glass birds used to be, his arms crossed over his chest and his face turning dark red. As for me, I was frozen in fear and could barely believe what I saw with my eyes and heard with my ears. Danny weighed only eighty or ninety pounds. Where had he found the courage to stand up like that?

"You don't listen good, do you?" the man said as, in a flash, he slapped Danny so hard across his mouth that Danny's head just about snapped off, nearly sending him airborne before he fell in a heap on the floor. "Maybe you'll listen better now."

Just then, the phone rang, which was weird because the phone hardly ever rang, and when it did, it was usually someone from Danny's school asking about why Danny wasn't coming to class; but now it was vacation, so there'd be no reason for anyone to call. The phone kept ringing, twice, three times, four times while Lucetta and I stood still, frozen in fear, while Earl watched over us with his chest thrust out and his fists bunched at his sides. Finally, after maybe a dozen rings, Lucetta lurched over and answered it.

"Hello?"

"Bitch!" Earl yelled, knocking the phone out of her hands.

"But Earl!"

"*But Earl, but Earl,*" the man mocked as he slammed the phone down. "I need you boys to leave," the man said, crossing his hands over his belly.

"No!" Danny said again, getting on his feet, throwing himself against the man, and pummeling him with his fists, with his head, with his teeth—the way he'd done to me, but worse. "No! Get out! Leave Miss Lucetta alone!"

I wish I could say that I joined Danny, fighting, but I was so scared I couldn't move. Danny thrashed around until Earl took Danny's hands, pinned them behind his back, and then, with his free hand, punched him. Once again, Danny fell onto the floor. This time he stayed there, his face going red and mottled like a dirty old sponge.

In the silence, we heard the birds singing: *Stop it, Earl! College boy! Stop it, Earl! I love you!* As they sang, they hopped around wildly, like they were trying out their new breakdance moves. *Stop it! Earl! I love you! Stop it, Earl! Quit! College!*

"Get out, boys," the man said.

Stop it, Earl!

Which was when it finally clicked into place: Those birds, they were like tape recorders. Earl had been over at the house before, had hit her before, had done—

"Out!" he yelled.

"Better do what he says," Lucetta said.

Me, I was already halfway out the door, dragging Danny behind me. Because honestly and truthfully? If there's one thing I knew I didn't want to stick around for, it was a beating. But once again, Danny flat out refused. He pulled and squirmed until he'd freed himself from my grip and, running back into the front room, yelled, "Get out!"

"That's how you want it, huh?"

"I'm not scared of you!"

"Not yet, you ain't."

SMASH! CRASH! SMACK! Earl pulled the birdcage from its usual place and threw it against the floor, where it rolled once or twice before coming to a stop in the corner. Next, he toppled the cabinet where Mamma's birds used to be, breaking all the mirror glass. He tore up Mamma's bedroom, breaking the windows and tearing up the bed. He kicked the TV set in. Grabbing a knife from the kitchen, he tore open the pillows on the sofa and ripped open the pictures on the wall. He even took the family photographs out of the frames. Went over to the kitchen cabinets and tore through them too. Then he was in our room, cursing the whole time, throwing things around. The man even busted up the Christmas presents that me and Danny had given to each other. And everywhere, where he ripped things open, out came money—dollar bills, fives, twenties.

"You keeping this for yourself, Lucetta?" he yelled, waving the money under her nose. "Huh? Huh?"

"Stop it, Earl," Lucetta begged from where she lay crumpled on the floor. "These boys don't mean nothing to you. Why you want to do them a pure evil like that? They're just children, Earl. Just two brothers trying to get by."

"You hiding something in here too?" he said, holding Bow-Wow by his scrawny neck.

"No!" Lucetta begged. "Leave that be."

But he didn't. He pulled Bow-Wow's head right off of his body.

Which was when Sonny stood up inside his upside-down cage, puffed out his chest, fluffed his feathers, and said, *Stop it, Earl!*

To this day, I don't know if Earl heard Sonny or not, but as Lucetta continued to beg, Earl wound down, like he'd run out of batteries, or like all the air had gone out of him.

"You done for," was all he said.

As for me, it was like someone had come along and poured concrete in my veins. I couldn't move at all. I could barely open my mouth. All that money had been my responsibility. It was Danny who broke the spell. "My doggy!" he said. "Look what he's done to Bow-Wow!"

"Get out of here," I said to Earl.

I didn't even know where I was, and if you'd have asked me what my name was, I wouldn't have been able to tell you. But the words came out anyway, straight and calm. The man just glared at me with his big eyes, the centers all black and glinting with yellow. Then he broke into a grin, and, putting his two hands up, like he was saying *just kidding with y'all*, said, "Well, yeah, little man. Guess it's time for me to be taking my leave anyway. Got business to attend to." And with that, he stuffed our money into his pockets, grabbed Lucetta's hand, and sauntered off like he owned the world, pulling Lucetta along behind him. From the next street over, I heard the sound of dogs howling.

17

PAPERCLIPS

"We won't ever see her again," Danny said.

"Probably not."

"Now what are we going to do?"

Truthfully, there wasn't anything *to* do but clean up the mess, calm the birds down, and put the busted-up TV out on the curb. So that's what we did, at least in part. Neither one of us had the heart to so much as look at what was left of Bow-Wow. And as for the torn-up sofa cushions and all the broken plates and glasses—there wasn't much we could do. We swept up as best we could, but there were so many pieces of broken *everything* that we could barely see what we were doing through our tears. When we climbed into bed that night, we were all but sure that we'd never see Lucetta again.

It was around midnight that we heard a thud, like a bag of garbage landing on the sidewalk, and jumped out of bed. Lucetta was lying in the doorway, half-in and half-out of the house. She wasn't moving at all.

"She's dead for real this time," Danny said.

"No, she isn't," I said, bending over and putting my ear to Lucetta's mouth. I could feel her warm air on the side of my face, feel the soft moisture there. "She's breathing."

"He tried to kill her."

"But she's alive."

"We've gotta call the cops."

That's when Lucetta spoke. "No," she said in a tiny whisper. "No police."

"But Lucetta!"

"No police."

"But he done near killed you."

"No police."

I love you! Stop it, Earl! I love you!

"The birds," she said. "They okay . . . ?"

Danny began to sob, and a moment later, I did too. We'd been crying so much, for so long, that I didn't think we could cry anymore, that we'd simply run out; I was wrong. As he held Lucetta's hand in his, I realized, for the first time, how much Danny had come to love her—and how much, in her own way, she loved him too. But he'd changed. His face was so thin and droopy and his eyes so dull, he looked like one of those kids in the "here's how you can help a hungry child" advertisements.

"The birds are okay," I said.

"How about Bow-Wow?" she muttered.

Hearing his name, Danny got up and went over to where we'd left Bow-Wow lying in pieces on the floor, picked him up, and threw him in the trash while Lucetta, lying on her back, watched through swollen eyes.

"Don't," Lucetta moaned. "I'll sew him back together."

"We've got to call 911."

"No police," Lucetta said again.

"What if he comes back here, looking for you? What then?"

"He won't come back. There's nothing to come back for."

She was right. Earl had pretty much wiped us out.

Danny and I looked at each other, and somehow, even without words, we knew exactly what we had to do. With one of us on either side of her, we slowly managed to haul her to the bed. Once she was in the bed, we took off her shoes, loosened her clothing, and—looking the other way, trying not to look at her where we shouldn't be looking—pulled her jeans off so she could be more comfortable. Then we cleaned her up as best we could, gently washing her with a washcloth, wiping the blood off. Eventually, her breathing became regular and slow, and she fell asleep.

That night, Danny and I both stayed up with Lucetta. But the next day, we were too tired to keep on like that, so we took turns sitting with her, giving her small sips of water, holding a cold compress to her head, to her cheeks, to her hands. When it was my turn, Danny curled up and went to sleep, and vice versa.

We lived off macaroni and cheese and Rice-a-Roni, and a couple of days later, when that ran out, we ate Cheerios and raisins.

"We gonna start starving again," Danny said.

It wasn't far from the truth. The kitchen cupboards were getting bare, and now, what with Lucetta having been taking her little bit here and there, and Earl stealing it all over again . . . it wasn't good. What was strange was how both of us avoided mentioning all that money that Lucetta had been stashing around our house. It was almost as if we'd known about it all along, known she was stealing from us, but didn't want to *know* know, so we never did ask. Another thing that we didn't talk about, but somehow had agreed on, was that despite all the bad things she'd done to us, neither one of us wanted to turn her out. The opposite was true. We knew if we turned her out, she'd be back on the street, and in no time she'd be dead for real.

"We'll be okay," I said. "We've still got *some* money in the bank account."

"How you know that? How do you know that she hasn't gone and wiped us out?"

"Bank statements," I said.

"How much is left?"

As I got up to get the bank statements, Cher and Sonny started up again. *I love you!* they sang. *Stop it, Earl!* And when, a moment later, I pulled out the banking box from under Danny's bed to discover that it was empty—no records, no ledger, no statements—I knew exactly what had happened: Earl hadn't just busted up our house and taken our money, somehow or another he'd gotten into our bank account too.

And Sonny and Cher—they'd known all along. If only I'd listened to the birds, then maybe we wouldn't be in such a terrible way.

"The bank statements are gone."

"What?"

"Miss Lucetta," I said, "what'd Earl do with the bank statements? How'd he get into our account?"

"I'm sorry, boys," she whispered.

"Couldn't you stop him?"

"He made me do it! He made me go in there and get it!" was all she said before lapsing into groans. Her breath smelled like sour milk. Around her eyes, her skin was getting yellow.

"What are we going to do?" Danny said.

The time had come, I realized, to make my own executive decision—and that decision was that we had no choice: we were going to have to sell Mamma's jewelry. It was a good thing I'd kept the very fact of its existence to myself, that's for sure, because if Lucetta had even been a little bit aware that maybe, somewhere in the house, we'd been keeping jewelry, Earl would have wiped that out too.

I beckoned Danny to follow me to the front steps, where Lucetta couldn't hear us, to tell him about Mamma's jewelry— how I'd hidden it away good and how, if worse came to worst, we'd just have to go ahead and pawn it.

"How do you know that Earl didn't take it when he was busting up around here?" he asked.

"I checked," I said. "It's still there."

"You sure?"

"Come on," I told him, and together we went back to the shed, where I showed him how I'd taped up Mamma's jewelry box inside another box inside the box of detergent. "See?" I said, handing it to him. "Shake it if you want."

He picked it up, shook it, and then shook his head.

"How much you think it's worth?" he asked.

"I don't know," I said. "Guess we better open it on up and see what we've got."

We slit open the tape and emptied the box onto the floor. What came out was paper clips. Mamma's jewelry was gone.

18

I MAKE A SECOND EXECUTIVE DECISION

Lucetta was getting worse and worse. One morning, she spiked a fever and lay there all hot, covered with sweat and groaning.

"We've got to call someone," I said.

"No," Lucetta murmured again and again, but it was hard to tell if she was responding to something we'd said or something that was going on in her own head, some scary movie that played without stopping. "No," she'd say. "No, no, no, no, no."

By the afternoon, when I came in to relieve Danny—we were still taking turns sleeping—there was just something different, something different and worse. For one thing, we'd been managing to keep Lucetta fairly clean, but now the whole room smelled like piss. There were stains on the bed-sheets. And Lucetta herself? She looked like Mamma did, the day me and Gabriel put Mamma under the house.

"We've got to call an ambulance," I said.

"But then they'll know that she doesn't belong here," Danny said. "They'll take her away, and they'll figure out we don't have parents, and the next thing you know . . ." He didn't even want to say it.

"They'll find out she stole from us," I said.

"I know."

"She stole just about all we had, even Mamma's wedding ring."

"But James!"

"She brought that man into our house. What if he had done to you what he did to her?"

"But if they come and get her, then what? They'll know something's wrong. They'll ask us who she is, and if she's our mother. They'll take her away. Maybe even put her in jail. Next thing, the social workers will be at our door."

"I know," I said. "But I'll think of something."

"No," Lucetta said.

But I couldn't just let her lie there like that—lie there and die. And then what? Danny and I would have to take her body out and shove it under another house? Plus, even if she got well, then what? Would she steal our clothes too? Sell our school books?

"I have to," I told Danny.

I got up, went to the living room, and dialed 911. The place still looked like a hurricane had hit it, but I just didn't have the energy or desire to clean it.

We packed a bag with some of her things—clothes, a hair-brush, a toothbrush, and even a picture of Danny and me, just in case she got lonely—and waited.

"What are you going to tell them, when they come?" Danny said.

"I've got it."

It was true; I had all kinds of lies prepared. I was going to tell the ambulance people that Lucetta was our cousin and that our mamma was a long-distance bus driver who was away on work and that Lucetta had come back to the house from doing errands all beat up. Sure enough, they asked right away: "What happened in here?" one of them said as he strode through the door.

But when they saw Lucetta, I guess they forgot all about the mess in our house, because they didn't wait for an answer. They just wanted to know how long Lucetta had been like that, how old she was, and if she was on any medication. Then they wrapped her in blankets and put her on a gurney and took her away. "You did the right thing, calling," one of the ambulance men said as he carried Lucetta out the door. He and the other man shoved Lucetta into the back of the vehicle, shut the door, and drove off.

"I sure hope she's going to be all right," Danny said before bursting into tears and burying his face in my stomach.

"Don't worry," I said. "They'll patch her up good. And me and you, we'll go and visit her."

It was only then that I realized that not only did we not know which hospital they'd taken her to, but also we didn't even know what Lucetta's last name was.

We called around anyway, contacting every place we could think of, mainly in Baton Rouge—Our Lady of the Lake, Baton Rouge General, Earl K. Long—because Crystal Springs is too small to have a real hospital. They all said the same thing: they couldn't help us unless we had a last name. "But you see," I'd explain, "she never did tell us. But her first name, it's Lucetta. Can't you look and see if you got someone named *Lucetta*?"

"The system can look people up only by last name."

"No one named *Lucetta* in the emergency room?"

"Sorry."

We talked about trying to find her ourselves—going to all those hospitals and looking around for Lucetta—but even Danny realized that the chances of our finding her that way were nearly zero. Who knew? Even if we found her, she could be so covered with bandages and casts that we wouldn't recognize her anyway. Our only hope now was that she would try to get in touch with us. But we didn't even have a phone anymore; Earl had seen to that. As the days passed, we realized that we'd never see her again.

I had a million worries—more worries even than when Mamma had first died. Because now, we didn't even have hope. Any minute now, the cops could be pounding on the door, demanding to know what all had happened. Or a social worker. Or who knew who? What if Lucetta had gone and told everyone at the hospital our business? School would be starting up soon, and Danny and me, we had to find a way to survive.

On the last day of the year, there was a knock at the door.

"James!" Danny said, peeking out the window. "It's some lady!"

"What does she look like? Does she look like a social worker?"

"I don't know," Danny said. "She's dressed normal."

I had to think, and fast, because even if she wasn't a social worker, she could be some kind of undercover cop. It could even be Mrs. Jessup, from school. There was another knock.

"What should we do, James?" Danny said.

But by then I had my story all straightened out: how our mother had visited a friend across town, and how Danny had thrown a temper tantrum, messing up the whole house, and on and on. I tell you, I could have written more books than all the books in the school library, and they would have been better than stupid *Lord of the Flies* any day. "Answer the door," I whispered. "But let me do the talking, okay?"

He opened the door, and I saw her with my own eyes: flowing long red hair, big earrings, and eyes so green that they looked like they were made of lime Jell-O. Something about her was familiar, but I couldn't say what. She was dressed in tight-fitting jeans and a woolen jacket, and she was downright beautiful. Danny was speechless, gaping.

"Don't you know me?" she said.

"Ma'am?" Danny said.

Rubbing the back of her hand across her eyes, the lady breathed a deep breath. "I'm Lila."

19

LILA MOVES IN

We stood stock-still on the front porch, staring. All three of us. It was like having a three-way, don't-blink, don't-talk, don't-breathe contest. Finally, Lila got all teary, fell to her knees, opened her arms, and calling our names, said, "I've missed you so much."

Again, it was the strangest thing. Danny and me had been on our own for so long that a part of me wanted nothing of her. Another part of me was so happy to see her that I didn't have words. Still another part of me wanted to hit her and tell her to get her butt back to Los Angeles. Another part of me wanted to bury my face in her lap and sob like a baby. But the part of me that came out was the part that said, "You've been gone a long time."

"I know."

"What do you want?"

But Lila, getting up, didn't answer. Instead, she got up and went inside. She looked at the broken cabinet where Mamma's glass birds had been, at the family photographs lying on the floor, the broken phone, the busted-up sectional. She walked over to the birdcage. *Stop it!* Cher sang. *Stop it! Stop it!* Then she looked at me and Danny.

"What happened?"

And just like that, it all came out, every last bit of it except the part about where Mamma's body was, because even Danny didn't know that, and didn't need to know it, either. We told her how when Daddy had gone after her, he'd had a heart attack, and how after that, everything started falling apart, with everyone worrying about her all the time, and Grandma dying, and how Mamma had kept on keeping on until she'd died too. We told her about Gabriel and his auntie, and how Gabriel was the one who had come up with the master plan. And then we told her about Lucetta and about what had happened to her. We told her about Bow-Wow. We told her about Mamma's jewelry.

"Oh God," she said, when we were finished. "Oh God. I'm so sorry, boys. I'm so, so sorry. Oh God. And you went and listened to that idiotic boy?"

"We didn't know what else to do."

She buried her head in her hands.

"Lord have mercy," she said. "You let Gabriel talk you into all that. Didn't you know that you two never would have been split up? They don't split up siblings, first, and second—"

"But you weren't here!" Danny interrupted. "No one heard from you at all, not in all those years! How we supposed to know all that?"

"But they would have tried to find me," Lila said. "First thing they do is try to locate next of kin."

"What?" I said. "But Gabriel said—"

"Gabriel! Gabriel isn't right in the head. Good God! What kind of nonsense was he telling you, scaring you stupid like that?"

Suddenly, I was ashamed, as ashamed as I've ever been— even more ashamed than the day we put Mamma under the house. "Are you going to call the cops on us, get us sent to JV?" I said.

She looked at me with her big, soft eyes filled with something so hot and terrible that it was like they were going to melt. But all she said was "No, sweet lamb."

I stared at the floor, hoping that she wouldn't notice that my heart was pounding so hard it was like someone was beating a tree with a stick. But Lila must not have noticed, because a minute later, sunk in thought, she said, "You said her name is Lucetta? Does she call herself Miss Lu?"

We nodded.

"Oh Lord."

We had a million questions to ask her, but something about the way she just sat there, rocking back and forth, as if she were her own baby, made us both quiet. Finally, she looked up and said, "We've got a lot to get straightened out."

"What about Zip?" Danny said. "Is he going to come too?"

Looking from me to Danny, and then back again, she said,

"I never did get married."

"But you moved to California!"

"I never went to California."

"What about all those postcards you sent?"

She hung her head. "Sent them from Shreveport."

"But they were from *California*," I said. "The postmarks said so—*L.A.* Isn't that Los Angeles?" But even as I said it, I realized my mistake. The postmarks hadn't said *L.A.*; they had said *LA*. Louisiana. But I persisted. "Where'd you get all those postcards, then?"

"I ordered them. Couldn't be easier."

"What you mean you've been living in Shreveport?" It was Danny doing the talking now, and he was furious. "You were in Louisiana all this time and never let Mamma know? We've been all alone and almost starving and you've been in Shreveport all that time?" As his entire body began to shake, he burst into a series of wild howls, howling and screaming like a wounded animal, until, finally, Lila pulled him into her arms.

"I'm here now."

After Danny calmed down, Lila started in on her story. There were lots of ins and outs and twists and turns, but what it came down to, in the end, was that when Lila had first run off with Zip, she really did think she was going to marry him and go to Hollywood. But what really happened was that he convinced her that the only way someone like her could get started was by working the "clubs"—and by "clubs" he meant strip clubs, places where she took off her clothes and danced while a bunch of men eyed her up and down.

"But Lila," I said, "you didn't have to do that! Why didn't you come home? Mamma and Grandma were worried sick. They went looking for you everywhere. They hired a private detective and everything. I don't understand. Why didn't you just get on a bus and come on home?"

"The thing is," she said, and now her voice was steady and low but so quiet I could barely hear her, and all one speed, almost like she was a robot talking and not a real person. "I really did love Zip. I believed everything he said. He told me he was going to get me onto the stage. And he said that dancing— doing like I was doing—was just the beginning. Said that we had to stick together. Said he was my manager. Said he was going to marry me. Kept telling me that our ship was about to come in. Said that he was talking to people in Atlanta, in Dallas, in Phoenix—all kinds of people he knew. He said I was beautiful and talented, but that I had to be patient."

"But *Lila*," I said, "that's just crazy!"

"I know that now," she said. "But I didn't understand that then."

"But . . ." I said.

"How old are you now, James?"

I told her.

"So you're old enough to know how things are?" She didn't wait for an answer. "He hit me. The first time he did it, I just kind of took it. But the second time he tried it . . . I went right to the shelter, to the women's shelter, because I wasn't going to get hit again."

"What has that got to do with anything?"

"The shelter, it's where women go, women and girls both, when they don't have no place else to go."

"You're telling me you've been living in some shelter all these years?"

"No, baby," she said, her voice dropped so low that I could barely hear her at all. "But what I *am* telling you is that all kinds of women end up in places like that."

"So?"

"I met someone named Lu there. Lucetta. Miss Lu. Little girl, she went around with some man named Merl or Ed or Burt or something like that?"

"Earl," Danny whispered, his voice filled with wetness.

"Yeah, that's it. Earl. But your Lucetta? She was like my big sister, in the shelter. She came in all beat up—straight from the hospital, as a matter of fact. It was because she didn't have any other place to go that they sent her to the women's shelter. Anyway, she kind of took me under her wing, gave me hope when I didn't have any. Then, well, the girl stole from me. Stole ten dollars. It wasn't much, but it was all I had."

"She stole from us too," Danny whispered, his voice filled with tears.

"But you see," Lila continued, "before she did me wrong, she did me right. She told me something I've never forgotten. She said that if I went back to Zip, it would be all over for me, that I'd never get my self-respect back. And for that, I'm grateful, because, well, I never did see Zip again."

"I don't understand! Why didn't you come back straight away—or at least let us know where you were!"

"I wanted to make good," Lila said. "I wanted . . . I didn't want to come back with my tail between my legs. I wanted to show you—show Mamma—that I could make it on my own, maybe even make it in show business, with or without Zip."

"In Shreveport?"

"I got a job waiting tables, at a Blues club. Thought maybe I'd break in that way . . ." Again, she let her voice trail out.

"But you didn't," Danny said.

"You're right about that," she said. "All I did was make tips."

"But Lila," I said again, "all this time, you didn't even let us know where you were. And then, all of a sudden, here you are. Why all of a sudden? Did you run out of money? Did you get into some kind of trouble and need Mamma to bail you out even though Mamma's dead and gone and we're never going to see her again?" I was on the verge of tears myself now, but I sucked them back down my throat.

"No, baby," she said, "I'm not in trouble. I even have a little money saved up. My sin isn't that I did wrong the way you're thinking. But I did wrong another way—my pride. I was just too prideful to come home when I should have."

"So what you doing here now?" Danny asked.

"I called, remember? And called again. All I heard was shouting. Shouting and screaming. And then nothing at all, because no one picked up."

Danny and I looked at each other, remembering how Earl had yanked the phone from the wall. My stomach hurt.

"Can I stay here?" she asked.

We both nodded.

"And you'll take me to Mamma's grave?"

I didn't know how to answer, so I didn't. Lila was home. For now, that was all that mattered.

20

I YELL AT GABRIEL

With Lila back, I'd nearly forgotten that there'd ever been such a person as Gabriel. It was as if there wasn't enough room in my brain for both of them.

But when school started up, there he was. I had so much on my mind that I didn't see him coming until he was right on top of me. Just because Lila was home, it didn't mean I had stopped worrying. In fact, in some ways I was even *more* worried, because though I'd been able to put Danny off the trail, I knew that eventually Lila would ask me again about Mamma's grave. And if she ever found out . . . ? It was too terrible to think about.

Before the first bell rang, I had a stomachache. I wasn't sure if I had enough time to get to the bathroom before class started, and was panicked, because I sure did need to go. It didn't help that the halls were so crammed with kids that getting through would be a nightmare all by itself. I saw Kia and a couple of her girlfriends hanging out at the lockers, cracking up, the way girls do. I saw Ms. Baker, our math teacher, duck into the teacher's lounge. At the end of the hall, I saw a group of kids trading high fives. Everyone seemed hyped up. Me, I just wanted to find the bathroom. But before I knew it, Gabriel was on top of me.

"IT'S OFFICIAL!" he shouted, picking me up off my feet. He was dressed from head to foot in New Orleans Saints clothes: Saints sweatshirt, Saints hat, Saints sweatpants. If they made Saints underwear and socks, he was probably wearing those too.

"Put me down," I hissed.

"NOT UNTIL YOU KNOW THE NEWS!"

Kids were staring.

"Later. I have to go to the bathroom."

"BUT I'VE GOT TO TELL YOU!"

"I gotta go!"

"I AM ONE HUNDRED PERCENT LEGALLY ADOPTED!"

Finally, he had my attention.

"What?"

"Auntie's adopted me! That's why I was so long getting back from New Orleans. I couldn't tell you about it before, brother, it being top secret and all that. All that paperwork! Going to the judge, going to the social workers. *Had* to tell you that we were just having fun, just going on vacation, just seeing the sights. But no, we were on *official business*, because what we were really doing was getting me adopted! Auntie made an executive decision. And now it's official—Auntie and me, we're a family!" He was so excited that he grabbed me again, and I could tell, by the way he was squeezing me and breathing hard, that he was fixing to tell me every last detail.

"Let go of me," I said. "I have to *go*." My insides were squishing around badly. I tried to breathe it out, but a hot cramp came along, piercing me so powerfully that it bent me in two.

"But James! Dude of dudes! Don't you see?"

I didn't have a clue what he was talking about. All I knew was that I could barely breathe. "Got to go to the bathroom!"

"But don't you see? It's finally officially official. We've been living up here ever since I ended up in the emergency room, back at the Charity, when I was just a little kid. They were going to put me back in foster care, but she took me instead, and we had to move on up here to Crystal Springs. But now she's adopted me, legally, and we don't have to hide anymore."

His words, coming faster and faster, meant nothing to me. "Now Auntie's my very own real-life auntie and I'll never have to get hit or yelled at ever again."

For a second time, he picked me up, enfolding me in those giant, beefy arms of his and squeezing me like I was a teddy bear. "I LOVE YOU, MAN!" he said. "YOU ARE MY OWN TRUE FRIEND!"

My stomach churned and burned, and just as he was fixing on squeezing me even tighter, I felt it happen: my insides let loose, a hot stream. I clenched down on my butt muscles, but even so, I could feel a drop or two land in my pants. It smelled so bad that even with all that commotion and all those kids pressing close, with the smells of perfume and deodorant and bath soap and new clothes and hair spray and gum, I could smell it myself.

"*Damn,*" someone said, passing by.

"Who let one?"

"Smells like a sewer around here."

"Somebody's gassing up the place for real!"

People were laughing and pointing at us, when a girl said, "Maybe it was old retard man there."

"Don't look at me," Gabriel said, finally putting me down. Turning to me, he then said, "JAMES? YOU STINK!"

I stared at his huge shoulders, his red lips, and his big, blubbery, stupid face. I stared at his short-cropped hair and the way he wore his clothes, all hanging off him. I looked at his enormous hands, and his thick pink neck, and his huge feet—feet like those of a giant duck, all floppy and flat—and said, "Leave me alone, Gabriel."

"I'm just joking with you, James."

That's when I lost it for real. I heard someone yelling from very far away, and as the yelling continued, the crowd of kids gathered around us grew. Then I realized that the yelling was coming from me. "It your fault, you big, stupid retard! You're a moron! *You* were the one who brought that junkie into our house! *You* were the one who told me that everything was going to work out! And now—look! EVERYONE'S DEAD!

Mamma's dead. Daddy's dead. Grandma's dead. Lucetta's probably dead too! That man came into our house and took everything. EVERYTHING'S GONE, GABRIEL! All our money! Mamma's jewelry! We're hungry all the time, and you just go around stuffing donuts into your big, fat face! And every night the dogs eat Mamma! Every night the dogs come with their sharp teeth and eat her! Because of you! I NEVER WANT TO SEE YOU AGAIN! DO YOU HEAR ME, YOU BIG, STUPID MORON? I HATE YOU AND WISH YOU WERE DEAD!"

I was screaming at him, tears streaming down my face. A moment later, I started hitting him too, hitting him as fast and as hard as I could. I no longer cared about anything—not about the stink in my pants, or the pain in my gut; not about whether or not Lila stayed or went; not even about Danny. I was in a kind of ecstasy, like a dream that's so good, so pure and perfect, that you never want it to end. I had so much energy that I never wanted to stop. My blows landed with a satisfying *slap, thud, umph.* I went for his nose, his lips, his ears, his belly, his knees, his shins. *Whap, whap, whap. Thud, thud, thud.* I swear to God, if I had had a baseball bat, I would have used that on him too.

And you know what that big, stupid Gabriel did? Nothing. He just stood there and took it, while kids watched, saying things like "That kid's about as smart as a cow," "Looks like a cow too," "Maybe with all that fat he doesn't feel it." Even after Ms. Baker pulled me off Gabriel, Gabriel didn't do nothing, his head hanging down. There was blood on his Saints shirt.

There was blood on the floor. "What's going on here?" Ms. Baker was saying. "What's all this? Who's dead? What's this about? James? Who started it?" I didn't answer, and Gabriel didn't even look up. "Okay, then," she said. "Enough. Both of you. We're going to go visit the principal."

"No," I said.

Behind me, some kid snickered. "Going to see old Jessup, the meanest woman in America."

"Move," the teacher said. "Now."

"Can I go to the bathroom first?" I said.

21

ALMOST DONE

Afterwards, I sat in the principal's office, where Mrs. Jessup said, "What happened, James? Gabriel? Why are you two boys fighting? And what's this I hear about someone stealing your money? And your mother, James? Where's your mother? I've been calling the house. Calling her work number, too, and they said she hasn't been to work in months. What's going on? Every kid in this school is talking, and we haven't even started the new semester."

"We got robbed," was all I could say.

"Gabriel?"

"Ma'am."

"Do you have anything to add to this story?"

"I only wanted to help," Gabriel said. "I wanted to help James and Danny stay together."

"James?"

"The man came and stole all our money," I said.

"I meant to help," Gabriel said. "I meant to do good."

"He yelled," I said. "He ripped Bow-Wow's head off."

"Bow-Wow? Who's Bow-Wow?"

"Danny's little stuffed doggie," I said.

Of course, that wasn't all I *ended up* saying—because in the end, just about everyone wanted to know what had happened. I told the story of Danny and me over and over again, not leaving anything out, even when I grew tired, and even when it all seemed like something that must have happened to someone else entirely. I told the principal, and then I told the social workers, and then I told Gabriel's auntie, and then I told five or six police. I told the pastor from Grandma's church, and I told bunches of Grandma's friends—old ladies and old men who came over with casseroles and bowls of fruit and baked hams, and sat with us. I told about Lila—how she had run away and then come back—and about how we had lost Lucetta and didn't know where she was, or even if she was alive. I told about the dogs in the night. In the end, I even told about where we had put Mamma's body, Gabriel and me, and how we had stood on that sagging old front porch and said a prayer. And when I was all done talking, they let us stay together.

As it turned out, now that Lila was back, we were legal. As Mamma and Daddy had owned our house free and clear, there wasn't nothing anyone could do but let us stay put. And anyway, by the time Auntie Joyce found out what had been going on, she kind of took over. That was her name, by the way: Joyce. Joyce Keyes. All that stuff that Gabriel had been dribbling into my ear? Every bit of it was true.

"She adopted me all legal and everything," Gabriel said. "And she doesn't have to pretend to be someone else anymore, either. We're good to go."

"You see," Gabriel said, explaining (and explaining and explaining and explaining, because no matter what, the boy did enjoy an audience), "one day my foster mother—Mrs. Chauvier—damn, she locked me in the closet for so long that when I come out, I was almost dead. But I wasn't dead. I was hungry. She had these chocolates, see? Sitting out on the plate. I went to grab one and ate it so fast I didn't even taste it. Ate another, and another, shoving those chocolates down my throat. That's when she hit me, *wham!* Over and over again. *Wham! Wham! Wham!* I don't know what happened after that, but the next thing I remember is waking up in the hospital, and my legs were in casts, and my head hurt like crazy, and Auntie's sitting next to me, holding my hand."

"She a nurse?"

"Not exactly," Gabriel said. "She's more like a health *aide*. Cleaning people up, changing bandages, helping folks go to the toilet, things like that. But there she was, like an angel, sitting next to me. Every night, if I had a bad dream or something? She'd come and sit with me. Then one night she told me to be real quiet, because she was going to take me home with her. She didn't make me. She just said that if I wanted to, I could go live with her. By then all my casts were off and I was eating and everything. Man, they fed me good in the hospital too! Chicken and gravy, hamburger steak—anything you wanted, almost, and I could have as much as I wanted. There were nurses and doctors coming and going and ladies coming by and giving me stuffed animals and all kinds of things. But I still had nightmares, thinking how I was going to have to go back to foster care. So when Auntie asked me, did I want to live with her? What do you think?"

He grinned his big old grin.

"That's why we had to come on up to Crystal Springs. Because what Auntie had done was against the law big-time. That's why she had to work nights, too, working in the Texaco station, because she didn't want anyone to know anything about her, just in case they were looking for her. We were, like, hiding out. But then Auntie got her a lawyer. She explained it to me. Auntie went to the judge and told him everything, and now she's my real mother."

"That's true," Auntie Joyce added—because most of the time, once Gabriel got going, she'd have to jump in, with little details of her own, little corrections, things that she remembered but he didn't. "I didn't see it coming myself, and that's the God's honest truth. But when I saw that little boy all covered with bruises, his legs broken, lying up in the bed like that, it was like God himself was telling me to take that boy on out of there and raise him up as my own. I thought I'd gone and lost my mind. Just for starters, it was illegal, what I was doing. I'd never stolen so much as a roll of toilet paper from the supply closet or a pen from the clinic! And now here I am, taking a child, a child who doesn't belong to me, a child who is no kin of mine, a child who has been abused and could well be sick, and leading him down the hall and out onto the street. I didn't know where I was going to take him or how I was going to make a living—I gave up a good job when Gabriel and I came up to Crystal Springs—but I've been blessed, and here we all are. Together."

"Amen," Gabriel said.

"Amen," Lila said.

"Amen," Danny said.

"Amen," I said.

College man! Pretty bird! Stop it! I love you! Cher and Sonny added, before bowing their heads together and finishing up with an *Amen* of their own.

Because in the end? In the end, it was a full house again. Auntie and Gabriel stayed up in that tiny house of theirs, but they were over so often that it was like they lived with us. Lila moved into Grandma's room. I stayed in the little room in back, and Danny moved into Mamma's room—him and his stuffed animals. Because now, even though Bow-Wow was gone and he was getting too old for them, folks had given him so many stuffed animals that they took up the whole bed.

By and by Lila got a good job, working at the dry-cleaning plant. She had to wear a bright-blue shower-cap-looking thing on her head and a bright-blue uniform, and she complained about the smell of dry-cleaning chemicals, but it was a steady job, and it allowed her to take college classes.

Auntie got a new job too. Now that she'd adopted Gabriel legally, she didn't have to work night shift at the Texaco anymore. Instead, she went back to what she *had* been doing, helping take care of sick people. She got a job at a new public clinic that had opened up smack in the middle of town, so she could walk there.

And that's how, in the end, we found out what happened to Lucetta. Auntie Joyce did some digging, and, one day, she came home to tell us that Lucetta was alive. But, she said, Lucetta had been beaten up so badly that her brain wasn't quite right anymore, and she'd never be able to live alone. So they'd found her some kind of special, state-run home for people who were too sick to look after themselves, where she could stay for free.

"Can we see her?" Danny wanted to know.

"Now why would you want to go visit someone who brought all that evil to your house?" Auntie asked.

When Danny didn't answer, Auntie shook her head real slowly, saying, "Okay, I see how it is. Okay, then. Okay."

When we first went down to the home in Baton Rouge to visit her, Lucetta would barely even talk to us, but just lay up in the bed with her back to us, staring at the wall. She was so skinny, you could see her bones. But bit by bit she began to get better, and when we came to visit, she'd sit up in the bed, talking a mile a minute, asking Danny how he was doing in school and asking me if I had me a girlfriend yet. The fact of the matter is, I didn't want to go visit her, not at first. It was Danny who convinced me, saying, "She needs us. We're the only family she's got."

The other people in the home were a pretty sorry lot—sitting around in wheelchairs and smoking cigarettes and staring at the TV set all day long and playing cards—but Lucetta didn't seem to mind. "I have three meals, proper, and all my medicine, and everything I need," she said. "You know, it could be worse."

We kept waiting for her to apologize, but she never did. Eventually she did tell us that she didn't mean to do us harm, she had just wanted to get herself enough money to get away from Earl for good, but it hadn't worked out the way she'd planned.

Gradually we stopped visiting her. Auntie said that that was okay. Auntie said that God works in mysterious ways. She said that Lucetta was doing the best she knew how to, and we'd just have to leave it at that.

22

MAMMA'S FUNERAL

The first saddest day of my life was the day that Gabriel and I put Mamma under the house. But the second saddest? It was the day that the city of Crystal Springs sent a team to go under that nasty old house and pull Mamma out again.

It was a cold day in February, the rain coming down in torrents and then stopping again, starting and stopping. We had gotten permission to miss school, but we didn't do anything all day except wait for Lila and Auntie to come back from the other end of the neighborhood to tell us it was over.

"There wasn't anything to see but a whole lot of dirt and a raggedy old quilt," Lila said.

"And your mother's bones can't hurt you," Auntie said. "Her bones are just bones. *She's* in heaven." I didn't know about any of that, but I did know that as Danny and I listened to her words, we just about broke apart inside. Danny was crying so hard it sounded like he was going to puke his own guts out, and on my other side, Lila was squeezing my hand so hard that I thought it would fall off.

Mamma's funeral was in the same church where Grandma's had been. They'd taken up a collection, to do it right, and her casket was covered with white roses. Afterward, we all drove out to the same cemetery where Daddy and Grandma were buried, along with all other kind of kinfolk who I never did know because they all died long before I was born. They put her in the ground all nice and proper, with a headstone inscribed "Here Lies Elizabeth Ruth Moore, Beloved Mother of Lila, James Jr., and Danny, Beloved Wife of James Moore."

Things are better now.

I still have nightmares about dogs, but not as much as I used to, and now, when the dogs come to me in my dreams, they don't bite so much. It's more like they're just curious and want to sniff. My stomachaches are mainly gone too. As for Danny? He dreams all the time: bad dreams and good dreams, flying dreams and fishing dreams. Sometimes he gets scared and crawls back in bed with me in my little room. Or sometimes he'll have a nightmare about Earl and scream in his sleep. When that happens, I hear him from my room, shake him awake, and tell him he's dreaming. "Earl's gone," I say. "And he'll never come back."

Leastaways, I sure hope he doesn't. But I'd never say that to Danny.

THE END.